JOSHUA

by

Frank G. Davis

First Edition, 2022 under ISBN: 9798414951919

SECOND EDITION 2023   ISBN: 978-1-954253-55-1

Published by Authors Wild imprint of Van Velzer Press

DEDICATION

This book is dedicated to three very important people in my life. Without their help, none of my books would have ever been published.

Alicia Davis

Alicia has been my wife for over 46 years. I depend on her for oh so many things it would take many pages to list them all. I want to focus on how she's helped me with my writing. First, she understands when I'm writing I'm not to be interrupted. When the words are flowing, I need to get them written down before I forget what I want to say. Second, she is the first person to read what I have written and corrects my misspelled words and punctuation. She also informs me when my writing is stilted or doesn't 'flow' right. It doesn't matter if I give her three pages to proof read or thirty, she drops everything and focuses on my writing and goes over the needed corrections with me. Most importantly, she encourages me to write, even if it means I end up ignoring her for hours at a time. Once a manuscript is completed, I make a point of spending what she calls 'quality time' together.

<u>David Davis</u> (Not Related)

David is a friend of mine who lives a block away from me. When I mentioned I was writing a novel, he was very interested in my work. I gave him a copy of a partial manuscript to read and review and he was hooked. He quickly became my beta reader. In addition to double checking for spelling and grammatical errors, we also discuss plot points and suggests ways to make the story stronger. Having a fresh pair of eyes reading the manuscripts is important. I depend on David to tell me if dialogs and narratives flow. I'm amazed how much effort he puts into improving my stories all so he can get a free book signed by the author.

<u>Trish Lewis</u>

Trish does it all. She does the final edit before the book begins the publishing process. I never realized how much work it took to take a manuscript and put it into a book format. She creates the front cover, puts together the book description for the back cover, and adds an author's page with pictures that show what a handsome guy I am. In addition, she also promotes the sale of other books I have written. Now, I have a better understanding of how many hats she has to wear to get a book published. Thanks Trish for turning out a finished product that I can be proud of.

INTRODUCTION

The Border Patrol vehicle sat on a slight rise above the desert plain with its lights off and the motor shut down. It was a hot summer night without any breeze and both officers sat quietly waiting with all the windows opened. It didn't help much; both men were sweating profusely.

The one on the passenger side was scanning the desert below with his night vision goggles. There was no moon this night and they were at least fifteen miles from Nogales, far away from the lights of the city. The driver checked his watch, then said in a quiet voice, almost a whisper, "Damn that El Jefe. He's a half hour late."

"Patience, Bull, he's a Mexican. They're never on time," his partner replied, also in a low voice. Sound traveled at night in the desert and they wanted to make sure no one could hear them.

Five minutes later, Bull's partner, Jake, whispered, "He's coming, just over that ridge, dead ahead."

"How many does he have this time?" Bull asked.

"Hard to tell at this distance, a dozen, maybe more. They're ten minutes out from the kill zone."

Bull snickered and replied, "More like the party zone."

Ten minutes later, the group stopped in a dry wash bed and waited.

"Do you have a positive ID on El Jefe?" Bull asked.

Jake could hear the excitement in Bull's whispering voice. He was a rookie and this was only his third encounter with a coyote. Jake wasn't sure he was going to work out. "Yes. I've got a positive visual and he's standing exactly on the coordinates I gave him. I count a total of fifteen illegal's, ten women and five men, four of the women look like teenagers."

"I can't wait. Let's get this party started," Bull said as he quietly opened the car door and began to slide out but Jake grabbed his arm.

"You still have your body cam on. Take it off," Jake ordered.

"Relax, partner. It's disconnected from the car recorder. I hooked it up to my personal recorder so I could replay the fun I'm about to have anytime I want." Bull pulled his arm free and left the car.

Jake got out of the car shaking his head. *This new guy isn't going to work out,* he thought to himself. *Too much testosterone and not enough brains.*

Both officers walked quietly down the hill and were within ten feet of the group when Jake spoke up, "Greetings Jefe. You're late," he said in Spanish.

The man jumped at the sound of his voice, *"Chingado, hombre.* Don't ever sneak up on me like that again. You scared five years of my life away."

"That's what you get for being so late. Did you forget your Rolex this time?" asked Jake.

"It took longer to go around the last site. I didn't want any of these new people to see the bodies of the last group or even smell the rotting flesh. It might have spooked them."

El Jefe turned to look at the men and women who had crossed the border with him and his two helpers. The illegals looked exhausted, both physically and mentally. They had not eaten and had only a little water for the last two days. Each of them had paid El Jefe three thousand dollars to come to the land of opportunity, to get a start of a new life.

Bull was inspecting them, seeing which women he wanted to party with, touching their breasts or their butts, looking for the 'prime stuff' as he called it. He'd seemed to have narrowed it down to three women. He had casually thrust his hand between the youngest one's legs and grabbed her crotch, just to see how she would react. She screamed and slapped his face. Bull slapped her back, knocking her off her feet and onto her back. He stood over her and began to remove his pants when Jake interrupted his fun.

"Bull, business first, then play. Get over here."

Reluctantly, Bull pulled up his pants and joined Jake and El Jefe.

Jake said, "So I count fifteen people at $3,000 a head that makes $45,000 total. We're going to take $25,000 and you get $20,000."

El Jefe began to protest but Jake interrupted, "I know what you're going to say. Our deal was a fifty-fifty split. But you were late and we have to get you to Nogales so you can get back to Mexico without other Border Patrol or ICE people finding you and your men. So, consider the extra $2,500 as a late fee with shipping and handling."

El Jefe was smoldering but no matter how much he argued, Jake was firm. Finally, he shrugged his shoulders and turned away. Bull quickly turned back to the 'wet backs' as he liked to call them, even if every river bed in this part of Arizona was dry as a bone. He began unbuttoning his pants as he walked back to the young girl still lying on the ground.

That's when they heard it. It sounded like a big truck. It seemed to be coming down the same dirt path the two Border Patrol officers had taken and they raced back to their SUV, Bull buttoning his pants as he went. El Jefe took his men and the immigrants and hid behind the river bank.

The lights from the truck came over a hill about a half mile away. The two Border Patrol officers stood by their vehicle, both with weapons drawn but hidden from view, waiting to see who was interrupting their business.

When the truck was about a hundred yards away they could see it wasn't a truck at all, it was a bus, a large yellow school bus. It came to a stop next to the SUV and the door hissed open. The bus appeared empty except for the driver. They watched as the driver walked down the bus steps and said, "Good evening, officers. My name is Joshua and I'm here to pick up the illegal immigrants and transport them to Nogales for processing."

Bull looked at Jake with a confused expression and began to speak but Jake waved him off. He stared at the driver for a few moments before speaking. The driver was a large, very large, black man dressed in body armor with not one but two, side arms, with a taser and pepper spray also on his belt.

"Who authorized this pick up?" Jake asked, as he eased the safety off on his Glock, still held out of sight.

The big man smiled and answered, "It was Jesus. Jesus was the one who authorized it." When Joshua said 'Jesus' he said it like the Spanish name (*hey soous*).

Jake thought for a moment, then said, "I've never heard of a Jesus in the Border Patrol."

"He's new to the Nogales area," replied Joshua.

Jake's gun came up fast but Joshua was faster. He put two bullets in Jake's head before he could fire a shot. Bull had forgotten to release the safety on his weapon and it cost him his life. Joshua shot him twice in the head and watched him fall to the ground.

Joshua walked by the SUV and went down the hill with both weapons drawn. He knew what was coming next. He slipped on his night vision glasses and easily spotted all three coyotes, two with assault rifles, one with a pistol. Before they could fire a shot, he killed them quickly. He returned his weapons to their holsters and took the money off of El Jefe's body.

He spoke in perfect Spanish in a voice loud enough for all to hear. "My name is Joshua. I am here to take you to safety. I have killed the men who were going to rape your women and then kill you all. I have food and water in the bus and I will return the money you paid to the coyote, the pig known as El Jefe. I know you have no reason to trust me, but I will not harm any of you. Please let me take you to safety."

One by one, slowly at first, they all came out of hiding and got on to the bus. The girl who Bull was going to rape was the last one. She alone came up to him and said, *"Muchas gracious, señor, por todo."* She took his hand and together they walked to the bus.

PART 1

CHAPTER 1

Sacred Heart Catholic Church—Monsignor O'Bryan

It was late, very late, when my assistant came pounding on my bedroom door. "Monsignor! Monsignor wake up please. We have an emergency!"

I awoke, quickly got out of my bed and put on my robe. I stumbled over my shoe that I had left on the floor but managed not to fall and opened the door. "What is this emergency, Father Sebastian?"

"There are many people outside the side door seeking asylum," the Father gasped. "What are we to do?"

"How many people, Father?"

"Fifteen in all, your Grace, five men and ten women. One of the women was assaulted by the coyote, El Jefe or one of his men."

"Bring them in and take them to our cafeteria in the basement. I will be with you in a moment." I closed the door, picked up my phone and made two quick phone calls, then hurried to the cafeteria.

As I had feared, they were all illegals, but as a courtesy, I listened to their story. And what a story it was. Two Border Patrol officers were shot and killed along with the notorious coyote, El Jefe and his two assistants. The killer brought them to the church, pounded on the side door waking up Father Sebastian but left before he opened the door.

All of the illegals thought the killer was a hero. He had saved them all from certain death, not to mention the rape of one of the women by a Border Patrol officer. The spokesman for the immigrants said their hero was a very large black man named

Joshua who drove them back to Nogales and to our church in a yellow school bus, giving them food and water on the way.

The nurse practitioner (NP) who served our medical needs *pro bono* arrived by the end of the story and checked them all out. The young woman who claimed to have been assaulted by one of the Border Patrol officers was checked out thoroughly but other than a few cuts and bruises, the girl was fine. The NP said the girl kept going on and on about how lucky she had been to have this messenger from God save her.

I helped Father Sebastian set up folding cots for all of them and had them lay down and rest. It took about five minutes and they were all fast asleep, exhausted from their harrowing experience.

The other person I called showed up shortly after everyone was asleep, except for me. His name was Roberto Sanchez, a detective with the Nogales PD. I retold the story and he sat quietly as I spoke. The only time his expression changed was when I mentioned El Jefe was killed. He arched his eyebrows and sat up straight in his chair. When I was finished, he remained silent for several minutes, then said, "I think it best if we don't make this public knowledge, at least not right away. I would like to return tomorrow morning and interview each one of them. Please let them know I will not turn them over to ICE. I just need to hear each one of their stories. Can you offer them asylum for a few days?"

Before I answered his question, I asked a question of my own. "What about the Border Patrol? Surely, they'll find out two of their officers were killed. Their cars have trackers on them, don't they?"

The detective nodded and said, "They will find out early tomorrow morning and begin their own investigation. If they come calling here, would you be able to say you know nothing about this?"

It took me a moment to figure out what to tell him. "It's a sin to lie and it's a crime to lie to the police. But perhaps I can be indisposed just in case the federal authorities come to call. Would that be sufficient?"

He smiled and said, "Yes your Grace, that would be fine. I promise you I will never tell anyone I was here or that we had this discussion. We both should be okay, at least for a few days."

He turned to go, but he stopped when I said, "Roberto, I have known you since I baptized you as a little baby, you come to mass regularly and contribute to the church in so many ways, I bless you for that. May I ask you one last question? Do you think what the young woman said, that Joshua was sent by God to save them, could that be true?"

He looked at me for a long moment, then answered, "It could be possible. God does work in mysterious ways. However, I think this was the work of a vigilante. We will find out someday. Hopefully, these people will find the opportunities they seek. See you tomorrow morning, Monsignor."

CHAPTER 2

West of Nogales, AZ—Chief Border Patrol Investigator

The helicopter made a high pass over the deserted Border Patrol cruiser and hovered at an altitude where the rotor wash wouldn't interfere with crime scene evidence. I looked back at the convoy of our forensic crew making its way down a long and barely navigable dirt path. They stopped well short of the cruiser so as not to disturb any tire imprints in the area.

We moved slowly to where the dead coyotes lay and landed the helicopter. All six of us climbed out and I walked over to our Medical Examiner (ME) who was busy examining one of the coyote bodies. He had been sent out on the first helicopter almost an hour ahead of our flight. I hoped he had some information for us.

"What have you got so far, Hector?" I asked as I walked up next to him.

"Morning Chief. They were all shot sometime last night, I estimate between two to three am. One thing I'm damn sure of, whoever shot them was the best shooter we'll ever see."

"Why do you say that?" I asked.

The back of the man's head was mostly gone but when Hector rolled the body over, there were two bullet holes in the man's head, one in each eye.

"All five of them had similar wounds," said Hector. "You ever seen that kind of accuracy?"

"Any powder burns on any of their faces?" I asked.

"Nope, none. These shots were made from at least ten feet. You know anyone who could shoot that accurately?"

I didn't answer right away but asked another question, "What type of weapon did the killer or killers use?"

"If you think they were killed with a rifle, think again. I found bullets at most of the body sites and they were from a .44 magnum. My bet would be an automag," answered Hector.

"What did the shell casings look like, were they all the same?" I asked.

"So far, we haven't found any casings. I think he policed his brass," replied Hector. Then asked again, "So what do you think, Chief?"

I stood up and looked around before answering, then said, "I think you're right, Hector. It looks like we have a single, inhumanly accurate shooter who killed five men. Two of those men should have been pursuing the other three, not fighting the same shooter."

The rest of the day went the same way, more and more puzzling. The scenario we put together from the meager evidence we found was this: The two Border Patrol officers were on stakeout anticipating the three coyotes were going to be coming to this area with illegals but before they could make the bust, the shooter shows up driving a very big truck whose headlights probably exposed the officers and their cruiser to the coyotes and their illegals. The shooter killed the officers and coyotes and captured the illegals and took them away in his truck. There was no evidence to suggest the illegals put up a struggle or resisted the shooter. After I saw the coyotes with their eyes shot out, I don't think I would have resisted either.

The only good news was the younger officer had kept his body cam running during the whole encounter. For some reason, the senior officer had disconnected his body cam which was a violation of his Standard Operating Procedures (SOPs). So that was a dead end. One thing bothered us all, why would the younger officer disconnect his body cam from the vehicle where the whole shootout could have been sent in real time to headquarters and backup could have been sent out. Instead, he had it recorded on his personal recorder. Perhaps we'll find out when we download his recorder later today back at headquarters.

One last thing that really bothered me was why none of their superiors had been informed of this stakeout. In fact, both officers were supposed to be off duty until this morning. I think we need to find out a lot more answers to our questions.

Later that day, back at headquarters in Nogales, a group of us sat quietly and watched the video from the junior officer's recorder. Most of us were stunned by what we saw. The bottom line was that the two officers had gone rogue and were working with the coyotes instead of trying to capture them. It was a bitter pill to swallow. I had worked with Jake for over a decade and believed he was a straight shooter. What a fool I'd been.

Thanks to our junior officer's recording we saw exactly what happened right up to the point when Joshua blew out their eyeballs. Thanks to Bull's selection process for his 'party time,' we knew there were fifteen illegal immigrants and we had close-up shots of their faces, at least the women. They would be easy to identify once they showed up. Of course, at the present time we had no idea where they were. We presume Joshua had loaded them onto the big yellow bus and took them somewhere, maybe Nogales or somewhere only God would know.

Speaking of Joshua, we have his picture from Bull's download and are currently running it through our facial recognition software. So far, we don't have any hits but it's only a matter of time

We got two other bits of information. One was the number on the bus which was supposed to be in the yard where all the Nogales school system buses were kept. We weren't surprised a search of the yard didn't find the bus. The manager of the yard was in the process of filing a police report that the bus must have been stolen.

The other was the knowledge that at least one other group of illegals had been killed or abandoned and left to die by El Jefe in the desert, close to where our existing crime scene was located. Search aircraft were sent to the location and two other sites were found with human remains. A total of thirty-three bodies were discovered but the coyotes, real coyotes, not the asshole coyotes like El Jefe, had pretty much consumed the remains. Land units were sent to the two new sites to recover as much of the remains as they could.

So, our new scenario is that a do-gooder vigilante killed the coyotes and the rogue officers and either resold the illegals or took them to some place safe. I was concerned our shooter may be some kind of high-powered coyote who was moving in on El Jefe's business. Only time would tell. Eventually, we always find out.

CHAPTER 3

Questioning the Illegals—Monsignor O'Bryan

Early the next morning, right after the 6:30am Mass, Detective Sanchez arrived at the church to begin his questioning. The illegals had risen early, eaten their breakfasts and attended the Mass. I followed them from the sanctuary back to the basement to find the detective waiting patiently at one of the tables. He stood as we walked in and waited for them to find a place to sit and then joined them.

I thought it best if I introduced Roberto and gave a short overview of what was going to happen. "Once again, good morning to you all," I said in Spanish. "Thank you for attending Mass this morning. I know you were all blessed by our Savior Jesus Christ. Everyone crossed themselves, even the detective.

"I want to introduce to you a friend of mine. His name is Roberto Sanchez and he is a detective with the Nogales Police Department." I sensed a wave of panic pass through the immigrants as I continued, "Please don't be concerned. I have known Roberto for all of his life and he is an honest and compassionate man. He has promised me he will not turn you over to ICE or the Border Patrol. So please try to relax. He just wants to ask you some questions about what happened to you. He would like to spend about fifteen minutes with each of you in private. If you would feel more comfortable, I will be in the room with you but only as an observer."

One of the women tentatively raised her hand as if she were embarrassed to interrupt me. I nodded at her and she said, "My name is Maria Gonzalez, I am the wife of Raul, raise your hand please." A man sitting two seats away from her raised his hand. "Sitting between us is my daughter, Lucita." Without being prompted, Lucita raised her hand. "I have two questions for the detective. Questions that everyone would like to ask you. Is that okay?"

I looked at Roberto and he stood and said, "Of course, Maria. Ask your questions and I will answer them as best I can."

Maria gave him a little smile, then said, "Thank you, señor Roberto. My first question: Is there any chance we can remain in America?"

Roberto looked directly at Maria and said, "The Monsignor and I are working to make that happen. But I must be honest, I cannot promise you it will happen. At the present time there are legal people working to get you asylum. If granted, you have to remain in the church. If you leave the church you could be deported back to Mexico. But if you stay in the church, the next step is to get you American visas. Since American police were involved with crimes against you, we think this could happen. We will keep you informed as we move forward."

Maria nodded her head, then said, "The second question: can we keep the three thousand dollars Joshua gave us?"

Both Roberto and I sat stunned for a moment. We had no idea the man had given them any money. Maria looked at our surprised expressions and buried her face in her hands and began to cry. "I thought you knew! I should have kept my mouth shut."

When I regained my composure, I said as gently as I could, "Maria, did Joshua give each of you three thousand dollars?"

She gave a brief nod of her head, then said through her tears, "Yes. He took all the money we paid to El Jefe and gave it back to us. For most of us, it was all the money we had. He thought we deserved a refund."

Roberto laughed loudly and said, "I agree with Joshua. You do deserve a refund. But please hide the money and don't tell anyone else you have it."

With Maria's questions answered, we began the interviews. None of the men requested my presence in the interview room. Several but not all of the women, had me join them. The detective was very non-threatening. It was more like a conversation between two new friends, nothing like the police interrogations I'd seen on TV. He told them he was recording the interviews because what they said was important and he didn't want to forget a single word.

Some of the sessions ran a little longer than fifteen minutes. We began the interviews at 8:00am, took a break at noon for lunch and finished in the early afternoon. After that they were free to watch television, read or just talk with each other. Some took naps. What they had gone through would have been traumatizing for most people. One of the side effects was fatigue. I let them sleep as often and as long as they liked.

About three in the afternoon, Roberto came out of the interview room and invited me to join him. He presented his findings to me and where he thought we should go from there.

He told me as far as he could tell, Joshua was just what he seemed. He protected all of them from death that evening, then brought them to the church to prevent them from being sent back to Mexico and gave them a full refund of the money to help them get started. He really appeared to be saint.

But there were still some very disturbing unanswered questions, like how did he know El Jefe was going to bring the illegals to that exact spot on that exact day and time? How did he know about the crooked officers? How did he know all the men and women were going to be sacrificed in the name of greed? How did he know where to get the bus or the weapons he used? How did he know the church would take the illegals in? The list seemed to be endless.

We both wondered what happened to Joshua after he'd dropped them off at the church. Was he still in the area or had he left the state to avoid capture. One of Roberto's friends who worked for the Border Patrol said they had a picture of Joshua and they were certain they would be able to identify him very soon.

When I heard that, I got up and went out into the dining room. "Excuse me please, did any of you happen to take a picture of Joshua before he dropped you off at the church?"

I knew it was a long shot. These people were very poor. I would be surprised if any of them had any type of phone, let alone one with a camera. I was surprised when the girl the officer had assaulted raised her hand and came running over to me. She showed the picture to me and Roberto. Roberto took one look and sank back down into his chair. "Oh my God! I know that man, I served with him in Afghanistan. I saw him die."

CHAPTER 4

<u>The Killer Revealed,—Chief Border Patrol Inspector</u>

"Good morning, Chief. It's a brand-new day."

I looked at Cindy and did my best to form a smile on my face. Cindy was a morning person and I wasn't, at least not until I've had a cup of coffee. I had just poured myself a cup from the office coffee pot but hadn't had a chance to take a sip before Cindy had walked into my office.

I was just about to take my first drink when Cindy said, "I've got good news. Well actually, good and bad news. Which do you want to hear first?"

I took a long sip and felt my brain start to come alive. I smiled at her and said, "Give me the good news first."

"The FBI's facial recognition software has identified our shooter."

I sat down and took another drink and replied, "That is good news."

"Well sort of good news, they have identified him as Caleb, not Joshua. The report says there's a ninety percent probability he's Caleb Brown."

"Is that the bad news? The shooter probably used an alias to make it more difficult to find him."

"No. Sorry Chief. The bad news is he's been dead for almost five years. He was a Marine, killed by an IED in Afghanistan."

Well that took the wind out of my sails. "So, another dead end. I guess the facial recognition software was wrong. Caleb wasn't our shooter. He's still out there, somewhere unknown but we'll find him eventually. You have anything else to brighten my day?"

Cindy nodded but she wasn't smiling. "The yellow school bus was found."

I perked up. "That's good news." I said.

"Not really," she answered. "The manager of the Nogales school bus yard says they found the bus in the yard. It wasn't parked in its normal spot so he called to cancel his theft report."

What a roller coaster morning and it was still early. "Call the manager back and tell him not to touch the bus. Don't wash it or clean it. I want a forensic team out there ASAP. Maybe the shooter left something behind. Tell the forensic team leader I'll join them at the yard."

I was at the bus yard ten minutes later. The forensic team was in route, so I showed my creds to the yard manager and asked him if anyone had touched the bus.

"Ordinarily we would've taken the bus to the wash rack and cleaned the inside but after I saw the sign taped to the door I backed off. I figured you and your men wouldn't want us disturbing any evidence."

"Sign? What did it say?" I asked.

"Better if you see it for yourself," the yard manager answered. "It's in the last row, on the left end of the row."

I told him to tell the forensic team to meet me at the bus, turned and walked briskly to the bus. *This just gets more and more weird,* I thought to myself. When I reached the bus I double checked the bus number to make sure it was the shooter's bus, it matched. However, there wasn't any doubt I had the right bus, the sign was where the yard manager had said it would be. It read: **To the Chief Inspector of the Nogales CBP. All others please stay out.** How about that, a courteous murderer.

I put the paper booties over my shoes and the latex gloves on my hands, pushed the door open and climbed the three steps into the bus. I stood by the driver's seat and scanned the bus interior. The first thing I noticed was the heat. All the windows were closed, and even though it was early morning, the Arizona heat made it uncomfortably warm. It would be over a hundred degrees before lunch time. I didn't notice anything out of the ordinary, except for the manila folder lying on the driver's seat. There was another note on the cover written in bright red letters. It read: **For the CBP Investigator's Eyes Only. These documents are confidential. Any unauthorized reader of the contents of this document will be prosecuted to the full extent of the special secrets law.** I let out a laugh. *What a sense of humor the shooter has,* I thought.

I heard the crunching of feet on the yard gravel and turned to see the forensic team waiting at the bus door, reading the message. "Come on in and get to work. It turns out our shooter is a joker as well as a killer."

The forensic team consisted of three people, two women and a man. They were very good at their job. They were wearing paper jump suits with hoods and plastic face shields, gloves and booties. I had what I came for and decided to return to the office so I could read the shooter's 'confidential' document in private. I said goodbye to the team and let them get on with their jobs. I knew they would have a full report for me by the end of the day. I couldn't wait to get back to my air-conditioned car. My shirt was already wet with my sweat. I pitied the team having to work in the oven of a bus. They'd be drenched before the day was over.

When I returned to headquarters, I locked the door to my office, sat down at my desk and began to read.

It said, "Good morning Chief Investigator, my name is Joshua Brown. The man your FBI facial recognition software found was Caleb Brown, my brother, my twin brother. Our father was a Baptist preacher in Alabama. His name was Moses. He believed strongly in what the Bible taught. My brother and I were named for the only two remaining Israelites from the millions whom God delivered from the Egyptian Pharaoh to enter the Promised Land. Everyone else died in the wilderness for their sins, even Moses.

Those who entered into the Promised Land were the descendants of those who died, except for Joshua and Caleb. They were allowed in because they always obeyed God's Laws. Always! My brother and I always did our best to do whatever God commanded us to do.

"Just so you know, I didn't murder those five men in the Nogales desert. I shot them in self-defense. If you check the body cam footage from the younger officer, they tried to shoot me first. They were just a bit slow. I have a right under our criminal law to defend myself just as I have the right to defend myself under God's law.

"I had orders from my superior to rescue those fifteen people at all costs. I was given the day, time and location where I was to be. I was told which bus to borrow, where I would find it with the keys under the driver seat and where to return it with a full tank of gas. I was told where the people I rescued could find refuge and I delivered all of them there. I always follow orders from my superior.

"I have been told by my superior this is just the first of similar missions I will be assigned to. Please don't attempt to stop me. I will always follow my orders, no matter what it costs. I hope you understand. I don't want to hurt anyone but no one will stand in my way of completing my assignments.

"May God be with you always as he is with me.

Joshua"

This case just got extremely interesting.

CHAPTER 5

Asylum is Granted-- Monsignor O'Bryan

I was sitting in my rectory after morning Mass when there was a knock at my door. I stood and opened the door to find Father Sebastian. "Your Grace, Detective Sanchez requests a meeting with you. He says it's very important he speak with you as soon as possible."

I nodded and told the Father, "Please have him wait in the basement interview room. Tell him I will be there after I change."

Ten minutes later, I walked into the room to find the detective pacing back and forth. "Roberto, you look troubled, may I help you? Please have a seat, coffee?"

He sat down and shook his head. "No thank you, your Grace. I'm afraid I have some bad news. I just heard from my friend at the Border Patrol. The chief investigator is visiting every church in Nogales for the illegal immigrants. He said the inspector received a tip that they're probably being hidden in one of the Nogales churches. It's only a matter of time before he comes here. Is there anywhere in the church you can hide them?"

Before I could answer, Father Sebastian came running down the stairs. He slowed when he reached the basement floor but walked at a very brisk pace towards me and the detective. "They're here, your Grace. The CBP Chief Inspector and several of his officers are in the foyer. They showed me a search warrant and want to speak with you...right away."

We left the office and started for the stairs but they were already coming down the stairs. I met them as they reached the basement and said, "Good morning Chief Inspector. Welcome to Sacred Heart."

He said nothing at first, instead shoved his warrant into my hands and motioned to his men to begin hand cuffing the immigrants. They resisted, of course, crying and complaining until the officers began using more force. Before it escalated any further, Detective Sanchez yelled in a very loud, authoritative voice, "STOP! EVERYONE STOP NOW!

Surprisingly, even the officers paused while the detective spoke to the immigrants in Spanish. "Please, my friends. Don't fight against these men, they will only hurt you. Let them handcuff you. This isn't over, they cannot send you back to Mexico without a hearing."

There was still crying and obvious sadness but they all stopped resisting and the officers quickly cuffed them all.

I turned to the Chief Inspector and said, "See what a little humane action can accomplish. Tell me chief inspector, do you speak Spanish?"

He shook his head and said, "I'm an American, I speak English. I don't speak Spanish"

"What a pity. Do you know that ninety percent of the Americans living in Nogales speak Spanish? It seems like you're the outsider."

The chief inspector had enough of me, he turned and yelled at me, "I don't want your pity…"

Before he could continue, a voice from the stairway said, "It's a shame you don't accept his pity. It's obvious you need it."

The chief inspector turned quickly and yelled, "Who the hell do you think you are? Officer, arrest that man for interfering with a federal officer."

The man came down the stairs and said, "And I'm a federal judge with a document signed by the Attorney General of the United States granting these people asylum in this church. Officers, uncuff these people. You're all ordered to leave the church grounds immediately."

He turned back to chief investigator and said, "Your warrant is declared null and void. I strongly suggest you join your men…outside."

Back in my room, I kneeled next to my bed and thanked God for his miracles. Two weeks later, the federal court judged because of the border patrol's complicity with the coyote El Jefe's murders of thirty-three people in the Nogales desert, the fifteen who were saved from a similar fate were issued visas which allowed them to live and work in the Nogales area. There was a good chance they would be able to apply for citizenship. They would have to comply with very stringent conditions but if they met them during the next five years, they would be granted full citizenship.

All this came about because one man stood up to evil men who committed evil actions. Some say he is a vigilante but in my heart, I believed he is a good man. This country, this world needs more men like him.

PART 2

CHAPTER 6

The Port of Portland--Terminal 6

A phone rang in the kitchen of a busy Chinese restaurant. The noise level was so high, it rang several times before Liu noticed it ringing. He finally saw the flashing light on his phone and answered it, "*Wéi.*"

"Speak English, please. Is this Li?"

"No. This Liu. You want takeout?"

The code phrases matched. The man on the phone said, "The container ship you're interested in has been delayed. It's currently just off shore from Astoria, waiting for the weather to change. The new ETA at Terminal 6 is now two days from now at 1800 hours."

The caller hung up and Liu went back to work as if the call had never happened.

The captain of the *Kobiashi Maru* sat in his chair sipping his morning coffee. The storm had subsided and his crew were anxious to weigh anchor and start their trip down the Columbia River. Looking out the forward bridge windows he could count seven other ships also waiting.

"Is this normal, Captain?" came a heavily accented voice from behind him.

"Yes, Kunitada San. I'm afraid it is," the captain replied to the owner's rep. Actually, he was the owner's son on his first major cruise. "I hope you survived last night's storm without too much discomfort."

There was a pause, before the answer came. "I am fine, Captain. Thank you for your concern. Since the storm is over, why are we not moving?"

"We have to get clearance from the Astoria Port Authority. It's like an airport. The planes cannot move until they get clearance from the control tower. Once Astoria releases us, we have to wait until the bar pilot comes aboard."

"I don't understand why we have to wait for a man from a tavern to join us."

The captain turned away so Kunitada wouldn't see his smile. "It's not that kind of bar. I apologize for not explaining. There are miles of sand bars that prevent a direct entrance to the mouth of the river. They tend to shift during storms which make it very dangerous to proceed without a very special person, called a bar pilot. They come aboard to guide us safely past the sand bars and into the Columbia River. The Columbia bar, also known as The Ship Killer of the Pacific, is responsible for over 2,000 ocean going merchant ships being sunk attempting to enter the river."

When he didn't hear a response to his last comments he turned around but Kunitada had left the bridge. Perhaps he wasn't as well as he had thought.

He heard the sounds of the helicopter's rotor as it began its descent onto the small landing pad behind the bridge. He turned to a yeoman and said, "Weigh anchor."

The yeoman answered, "Aye aye Captain, anchors aweigh."

Once the ship had entered the river, it stopped briefly to let the bar pilot off the ship to be replaced by the river pilot who would guide them 75 miles up the river to the Port of Portland, Terminal 6. ETA 1800 hours.

The twelve hour trip upriver was uneventful. When they arrived, tugs were used to guide the *Kobiashi Maru* into Berth 605 where it was secured to the dock. It took two tugs over an hour to maneuver the 900-foot-long ship into position against the bumpers without damaging the ship or the dock. Long, thick, rope cables were used to hold the ship fast against the flow of the Columbia River.

As soon as the ship was secure, four monstrous cranes began moving into position to begin removing the majority of the 5,000 containers from the ship. The rest of the containers would be off-loaded at other ports along the river.

A gangway was put in place and the first person to come aboard was the supercargo, a man in his late fifties who was responsible to make sure only the containers intended for Portland were off-loaded and where they would be destined. His counterpart on the ship was the third mate, a Japanese man who spoke perfect English. The third mate and the supercargo had been friends for years. Once the two men agreed, the off-loading began.

Railway tracks ran parallel to the dock with special flatbed cars waiting for their containers to be delivered as far away as the mid-western states. Other containers would be directly loaded onto the trucks for delivery throughout the states of Oregon and Washington. Still others would be stored in the massive outside storage facilities at Terminal 6 to have their contents removed from the containers and driven away in smaller vehicles. Once all the correct containers were off-loaded, new containers were taken aboard the ship for delivery to ports in Asia.

CHAPTER 7

Tour of Terminal 6—Perry Hendrix

"Good morning. My name is Perry Hendrix and I'll be your guide for your tour of the Port of Portland's Terminal 6." I looked over the group of about twenty people standing in the lobby area of the headquarters building. "We will be using the same bus for your tour that brought you through the main security gate. Please be sure to keep your temporary security badge visible at all times. If you lose it, one of our security people will have to shoot you in the head and dump you in the river."

I paused for a beat to see their reaction to my joke. Most of them laughed or giggled, a few looked momentarily shocked, only one man, a large black man standing at the back of the group had no reaction at all. "Sorry, just a little bit of twisted humor but security is very important to us here at the terminal. There are literally millions of dollars of assets passing through the terminal every day. Our security people are the best there is, they are former police officers or prior military police. We're concerned not only with potential theft but also terrorist threats."

A lady in the front of the group raised her hand. "Yes ma'am, do you need to use the restroom or do you have a question?"

She blushed at my joke and said, "A question. I took care of the bathroom break earlier. Have you had any actual terrorist attacks?"

"Excellent question. Unfortunately, I'm not allowed to go into details but we get several threats every month. Most of them are pranks, but we have had three actual attempts to breach the security perimeter of the terminal since the terminal began operations. None were successful. The last one was an attempt to sink one of our car carrier ships that was unloading Japanese-made cars to our huge car storage area."

I glanced at my wristwatch and said, "Okay enough about security, let me get on with my brief presentation. Terminal 6 is the newest of the Port of Portland's terminals and contains all the newest features of any port on the west coast. Six handles a wide variety of cargos from every class of merchant ship currently in operation. Just to name a few of the classes of ships that dock here are car carriers, bulk carriers and container ships. The container ships are as big as a navy aircraft carrier and take up to a week or more to unload their containers and then load new containers bound for both domestic and Asian ports. During our tour today, we will see a Japanese ship that arrived yesterday from Singapore. You will see the giant container cranes unloading the containers and placing many of them on the special railway cars that run on tracks next to the ship. Others will be moved to our container storage area."

I saw the tour bus driver motioning to his watch. "Okay everyone, it's time to board our bus and begin our tour."

We have several tour buses of various sizes. The smallest have a fifty-person capacity; the largest, a hundred. Since it was the middle of the week with a small group, we took the small bus. The buses are designed for touring with glass roofs to allow for great visibility. Much of what we would see was only visible through the roof. No one was allowed to leave the bus during our thirty-minute tour. During that time, we covered almost all of the 419 acres of the terminal.

Our tour began at the east side of the terminal. "We have two enormous parking lots for import and export cars. The eastern most lot is for temporary storage of cars imported from Asia. The cars are brought in on ships designed to carry up to a thousand cars. The import cars are driven off the ship into our lot to await transport by rail or truck to dealers throughout the Pacific Northwest. This lot can store over 10,000 cars at one time."

We drove through the lot, saw row after row of brand-new cars. We stopped for a few minutes next to a large ship shaped like a five-story building laying on its side and watched car after car driven off the rear of the ship and into the lot. It reminded me of a line of ants marching to an ant hill. It seemed like it would never end but we needed to move on.

We didn't cover the western most lot since there weren't any ships loading or unloading there. After you've seen one giant parking lot, there was no point in seeing another one. The only difference was the west lot also stored Ford cars which were to be exported to Asia.

We briefly drove through our intermodal yard where a variety of cargo was stored awaiting pick up by rail or truck or to be loaded aboard an outbound ship. We ended up at the container facilities and storage yard. "Ladies and gentlemen, you're in store for a treat today. The ship you see is the *Kobiashi Maru,* one of the largest container ships afloat. This ship was due in several days ago but a storm off the coast delayed their arrival. As you can see, there are four giant container cranes working to unload the containers. Two of them are loading containers directly onto especially designed railroad cars. The other two are placing the containers on the dock to be picked up by container carriers and moved to our 125 acres of container storage. The carriers can stack containers three high. The yard also supplies hookups to refrigeration systems if needed."

We watched the unloading process for another five minutes, I noticed several people looking through binoculars to get a better view of the operations. A few were taking pictures or videos. One man, the large black man who didn't smile at my jokes, had a camera with a huge lens and was snapping pictures of the containers as they were taken to the storage yard. The tour was over and the bus dropped me off at the headquarters building, then took the tourists out to the security gates where their badges were collected. They walked through the gate to their cars and drove away.

CHAPTER 8

The Slave Trade

"**W**hat's happening?!" screamed the young girl in Vietnamese.

Her older sister pulled her close to comfort her. "Quiet, Moon. There is nothing to be frightened of. I think our box is being taken off the ship. Just sit next to me and hold on. Don't let the evil men hear you screaming."

Jade felt Moon snuggling close to her and she pulled her sister even closer. She could feel her ribs through the girl's torn and filthy T-shirt. She was wasting away, barely more than a skeleton. She placed her other hand on her sister's forehead. She felt hot. The fever had been with her for almost a week now. She said a silent prayer that God would save her and Moon but she didn't think either of them would live much longer.

It had all been so different before the men came. Their mother and father had been farmers in a small village near Ho Chi Minh City. They were very poor. When Moon was born, things got worse. That year the men came and said they were from the government and the families were to 'donate' half their rice crop to their leader.

There was barely enough to feed her mother, father and three older brothers. Many nights she got only a tiny amount to eat, not nearly enough. Then Moon came along and her parents became desperate. Her father had to steal food for them to survive but nobody in the village had much to steal. He began hunting but all he ever managed to kill were rats. Many meals were without rice, just weeds and rat meat.

By the time Moon was ten, one brother had died from a sickness, another had run away. When the two men from Ho Chi Minh City arrived in their village, they offered money to several families to buy their children. They promised the children would be well taken care of. Very rich Vietnamese families in Ho Chi Minh City had no children and were willing to pay money to adopt the boys and girls, they said. It wasn't a difficult decision for their parents. The next day they were on a small bus carrying all they possessed in one small plastic bag. There were ten children in all, three boys and seven girls. Moon was the youngest, the oldest was a girl who was in her late teens. There was a boy from their village who was thirteen. They didn't like the boy, he wasn't a nice boy.

When they got to the city, their little bus drove directly to the docks on the Saigon River. There were several other small buses waiting at the dock too. They were given some rice and a little fish, the first real food they had eaten in weeks. They were also given some tea to drink. They were all very happy, then they found out the men had lied to their parents. They were going to put them on a boat to sail to Singapore. That's all they were told.

Very late at night, a boat arrived at the dock and five evil looking men grabbed the children and forced them onto the boat. It turned out the men not only looked evil, they were really evil, very evil. Most of the children were silent as the boat left the dock and left the city behind, a few were crying.

There were about forty children in all, close to thirty were girls. It took three days sailing across the South China Sea to reach Singapore. They were all made to stay on the open deck at the back of the boat. By the second day, the evil men began paying lots of attention to the oldest girls, Jade thought the oldest was sixteen. The men kept hugging the girls, kissing them on the mouth and trying to touch their private parts. Of course, the girls resisted but that just made the evil men laugh.

On the evening of the second day, the evilest of the men grabbed the oldest girl and lifted her high off the deck of the ship. He had grabbed her by her bottom and he began kissing her breasts through her shirt. She struggled and screamed. Finally, in desperation, she clawed the man's face with her long fingernails, one finger raking across the man's eye.

He immediately dropped the girl who fell to the deck and crawled away as the man raised his hands to touch his face. He ran to the girl and kicked her several times, screaming at her in Chinese. The girl struggled to her feet and bowed to the man in submission. The evil man stepped forward and grabbed her T-shirt and ripped it off exposing her breasts to his touch. She didn't fight back or even resist. Instead she stepped forward, placed her arms around his neck and kissed him on the mouth in a passionate kiss. The evil man stiffened at first then began returning her passionate kiss. Suddenly, he froze, began screaming into her mouth as he tried to push her away but she held on tight, her mouth locked against his. With her face still pressed against his, she took a half step back and thrust her knee into the evil man's groin which caused his knees to buckle. She released her hold on him and he sunk to the deck moaning in pain, his mouth a bloody mess. The girl stepped forward and spit his severed tongue onto his writhing body. As a parting gesture, she quickly stepped between the evil man's legs and stomped down on his groin, not once but twice. She looked up as the other evil men began to rise. She turned her head and briefly smiled at the other children, then turned and ran to the side of the boat and dove into the sea.

The evil men didn't try to rescue her, nor did they come to the aid of their companion. Instead they sat on the opposite side of the boat and waited. After a few minutes, another Asian man came from the boat's wheel house. He walked directly to the evilest man and began screaming at him in Chinese. After a moment, he stopped screaming, stepped back, pulled a pistol from his belt and shot the man twice in his head. He said something to the other evil men and two of them stood up, picked up the body and threw it over the side.

The shooter turned and bowed to the children, then returned to the wheel house. The other evil men never approached the children again, except to bring them food and water. The evening of the third day, they arrived in Singapore.

CHAPTER 9

From Singapore to the Port of Portland

They arrived in the middle of the night at a dock in Singapore. They were 'encouraged' to remain silent and to climb up the ladder from where the boat was docked to a road where a very large bus was waiting for them. There had been several other boats like theirs docked next to them. When they got onto the bus it was almost full.

Jade noticed their boat left quickly just as the bus door swung closed and they began moving down the road. It was dark in the bus and everyone was tired, many were already fast asleep when a light at the front of the bus came on. A recorded message began playing first in Chinese, then in several other languages Moon and Jade couldn't understand. Then in Vietnamese it said, "Welcome travelers, we hope the first part of your journey was enjoyable and that you were treated well by the crew on the boat. Unfortunately, some of the boat crew members don't follow all our instructions. We apologize for any problems you may have had.

"We are currently traveling to a much larger ship that will take you all to America. Isn't that better than Ho Chi Minh City? Of course it is! There you will all be adopted by rich American families. It will take us three weeks to cross the ocean but unlike your recent boat trip you will be treated with respect by the ship's crew.

"Our bus trip will take almost an hour, so sit back and sleep until we arrive. There is a bathroom in the back of the bus if you need one. I'll wake you when we get there."

An hour later, the overhead light of the bus began to glow softly and music began to play. After several different Asian languages, the recording said in Vietnamese, "It's time to wake up. If you need to use the bathroom, there are portable toilets on the dock. Please use them now, it may be awhile before you will be near a bathroom again."

Moon and Jade joined the line in front of one of the toilets. When they were finished, they joined another line leading to five large metal containers. Each container had doors on the end which were wide opened revealing wooden crates on each side with a narrow walk-way between. There were two or three adults lined up in front of each container calling out names. When Jade heard a woman call out in Vietnamese, "Jade and sister Moon from Ho Chi Minh City." She smiled and took Moon's hand and hurried to the lady by the third container.

"I am Jade and this is my sister Moon. We're from a farm near Ho Chi Minh City. Are we the ones you are looking for?"

The young woman smiled at them and nodded her head. "I am called Pearl. I will help you get settled. You and your sister are the first ones to come to my container."

Pearl handed both girls a large bag and they walked up the ramp into the container. They had to turn sideways to move between the crates which went all the way to the top of the container. The girls were confused. Why were all these crates here but after no more than ten feet they came out into a large area which had bunk beds for up to thirty people, a real bathroom with both a sink and toilet, a small kitchen with a refrigerator and a stove. Best of all, it had a large television screen hanging on one wall. It was the most beautiful place they had ever seen!

Pearl said to them, "When the others get here, I will go over the rules everyone will have to follow until our ship arrives in America. In the meantime, please select your beds. You have first choice since you were the first ones here. I have to go outside now to find the others who will be living with you during your cruise."

While they waited, Moon began digging into the bag Pearl had given her. She squealed with delight when she found new clothes, two shirts, two pants and two pairs of underwear, two pairs of socks and matching slipper shoes. Besides the clothes she found a toothbrush, toothpaste, a bar of soap and a hair brush. The last item in her bag made her squeal even louder. It was a little brown and white stuffed bear. She was so happy she began crying. Jade cried with her, at last they were being treated like real human beings. Even their parents hadn't treated them so well. Jade said a silent prayer this would never end.

Within an hour, Pearl had brought in twenty-six more people to their container. Several of them had been with them on the boat from Ho Chi Minh City. They seemed as shocked by their new surroundings as they had been. The others they hadn't met were also from Vietnam, so they all spoke a common language. As the newcomers arrived, they chose their beds and went through their gift bags. Many of them also cried for joy.

Ten minutes after the last person came in, Pearl came in to give them their instructions.

"Everyone is here. Have you all chosen your beds?" Everyone nodded their heads. "Everybody gone through the bags? I want to make sure your clothes fit. Did all the younger children get their teddy bears? Hold them up so I can see them."

Moon and three other young children held up their teddy bears and wagged them back and forth, making roaring bear sounds. At least that's what she thought they were supposed to sound like.

"Okay, let's get down to business. Right after I leave the container, the hatch will be closed and locked for security and your safety. Later tonight, all five of the containers will be loaded on board a very big ship. This loading process will take most of the night and it could get noisy. The ship you will be on has thousands of containers. It doesn't usually carry passengers but on special occasions they will use these people containers. Out of the thousands of containers they may have no more than a few hundred people containers. Why do we use these to send you to America?

Because it's the cheapest way to travel across the ocean. It's the only way we can afford to get you to your new home.

"As I mentioned to some of you, it will take about three weeks to cross the ocean. Once we are loaded aboard the ship it will take a couple of days before we can open up the container. We will only be able to open it up for an hour each day, either in the early morning or late evening. There won't be much room to move around in and there won't be much to see. We will be surrounded by containers on all sides.

"Meals will be brought in to you twice a day and we will have access to showers once a week. Lights will go out at ten and come on at six the next morning. The television will show a series of prerecorded programs so there shouldn't be any fighting over what to watch. To listen to the programs, you will need to wear ear phones…"

Pearl continued to speak for a few more minutes before her phone beeped. She looked at the screen and said, "They're getting ready to load the containers now so we have to close the doors. As soon as the doors are closed the lights will go out so get into your bed as soon as possible. I know it's the middle of the night so I'm sure all of you must be exhausted. I hope you have a great trip."

She quickly turned and slid out between the crates, the container doors clanged shut a few minutes later. A few minutes after that, the lights went out. Thankfully, there was one dim night light.

Pearl was right, they were exhausted. Everybody managed to crawl into their beds before the lights went out. A few minutes later, Moon joined her sister. Jade pulled her close and found the teddy bear sandwiched between them. They were so tired, neither of them noticed when the crane picked up their container and placed it on the ship.

The first few days passed slowly. The doors to the container remained shut and locked. The children made their own meals from the food in the large pantry and watched a lot of television. The first thing they all watched was videos of them loading all of the many containers onto the ship. There was no sound only the picture but it was still very interesting. Some of them thought it was their ship and their containers in the pictures, others thought it was just a recording of some random ship being loaded.

After about fifteen minutes, the picture changed and showed the ship getting ready to leave the Singapore dock. Dock workers were removing the very large ropes that held the ship in place. The next scene was of little boats pushing the ship away from the dock. They watched as the ship began to move away from the dock by itself. Then the television went dark. At first, they thought it broke but a few seconds later a cartoon show came on. The small children squealed with joy, grabbed their teddy bears and sat on the floor to watch the show.

On the third day, early in the morning, the container doors were opened and Pearl came in. "Good morning, everyone. Are you all okay? In a few minutes we will be going outside for about an hour but first there are few things I need to tell you that I didn't get a chance to say to you earlier.

"Today we will begin the meal service. Someone will bring in a breakfast and a dinner, one for each of you. That same person will restock your pantry, check your bathroom, and refill your drinking water supply. It would be best if you sat on your bunks while all this is going on. Don't try to speak to the service person. They don't speak Vietnamese, so they won't understand you anyway. Any questions?"

There were none. Pearl continued, "The last thing before we go outside: does everyone see this large red button?" She pointed to the red button on the wall of the crate on the left side of the passageway. "You push this button for emergencies only. Under no circumstance do you push it for anything else. You push it if someone gets seriously hurt or sick. Getting a hangnail is not a serious injury and having a headache isn't a serious sickness. Don't push it if you're out of your favorite snack or tea. If you do, you will be removed from this container and you will have to spend the rest of the trip alone somewhere else on the ship. Does everyone understand?"

Everyone nodded their heads, the smiles disappearing from their faces. Moon looked like she was about to cry.

"All right, lets form a line and follow me outside. Once outside, please stay with the group. Don't go exploring."

When the children stepped into the sunlight, it took a few minutes for their eyes to adjust to the brightness. When Jade could see, the first thing she noticed was they were surrounded by other containers, four stories high, all painted different colors. She turned to look at their five containers and noticed they were painted blue, then she was shocked to see more containers stack on top, also four stories high. There was about fifty feet of empty space in front of the five human containers and everyone was milling around, checking out the area. They were placed so close to each other Jade wondered how anyone could get between them. She heard one of the older boys from her home container say, "Look, I found a path. This must be how they bring in the meals."

She looked where the boy was pointing and moved to look up the path. The boy was right, as soon as she looked she saw men pushing what must have been the food carts in front of them. The men were all Asian, probably Japanese, none were smiling.

Everyone got out of the way as the men pushed their carts up the ramps to the five containers. In less than ten minutes they all came out and returned the way they came.

After a few minutes wandering around in the open space, chatting with their neighbors from the other containers, trying to make new friends, they were ushered back inside. The doors clanged shut and they went to eat their breakfast.

For the next few days everything went well, the food was good and the living space was cleaned every day. They watched television, those who could read, selected books provided on a shelf near the pantry. Jade would read to Moon sometimes but mostly the younger sister played with the teddy bear.

By the end of the first week they had settled into a routine, then that changed. They had been outside expecting the men to deliver their breakfast meals but they didn't show up before they were told to go back into their containers. Many of them were hungry and began to look at the pantry to find something to eat.

Suddenly, they heard the doors being unlocked, then unbolted and finally clanged open. The man stopped his cart in the middle of the room and gestured for them to come get their breakfasts as he began cleaning the counters and restocking the pantry. They all sat on their beds and ate their meals as he mopped the floor. One small girl had only eaten a few bites before she jumped off her bed heading for the bathroom. In her haste she knocked the plastic meal container off her bed onto the freshly mopped floor. Before she could get to the bathroom, the man scooped her up and sat her near the leftover food. He pushed her face toward the food and made her eat it off the floor. The girl was terrified but she ate everything before the man released his grip on her neck. She stood on shaking legs and fell into her bed crying softly, clutching her teddy bear to her chest while her brother held her close. When the man mopped up the remains of the spilled meal, he continued into the bathroom. When he was finished cleaning, he picked up all the empty meal boxes, his cleaning tools and left without looking at any of the children.

As soon as they heard the door latched and locked, the girl's brother walked quickly towards the large red button. Almost everyone shouted at him, "NO! Don't push it!"

Two of the larger boys grabbed him before he was halfway across the room, speaking softly to him. They guided him back to his sister where he sat holding her hand but his eyes were on fire with hate. One of the boys returned to stand guard over the button while the other spoke to the group.

"We must be very careful here. None of us want to lose the chance to live a good life. Think about what happened from the man's side of it, the meals were late so he had to clean with all of us here which made it more difficult for him. Then, when he had just finished mopping, little sister jumps down and messes up his clean floor. So, he punishes her, making her eat the food she wasted. He didn't strike her or injure her. He embarrassed her and she lost face with us. Let me ask, how many here haven't been punished by our parents for something similar? How many have carelessly spilled a cup of tea or dropped a rice bowl on the floor. I cannot count the number of swats to the back of my head my father gave me when I was little sister's age. But I learned to be careful, just like I am certain little sister will learn."

The young man looked at the little girl wiping away her tears. She looked back at him and nodded her head.

"What do you say, younger brother? Is what happened to your sister cause enough for you to throw away this opportunity for all of us?"

The younger man stared back, then the fire in his eyes went out and he hung his head and said, "You're very wise, older brother. I will not push the button."

Everyone gave a great sigh of relief the incident was over and things could return to normal. Only they weren't to see normal again, not while they were on the ship, in their own little prison.

It began slowly, an occasional missed meal or forgetting to restock the pantry, the discovery of a rat in the bathroom. Then it got worse. First it was the shouting at the children, followed by shoving, then being tripped or pushed to the ground. The girls had it worse. Now, instead of one man showing up there was always two, two evil men who thought Vietnamese girls were sub-humans who existed only for the pleasure of men, real men.

When Pearl showed up, they were afraid to tell her what was happening. Those with injuries found a way of hiding it, bruises were covered as were cuts. But Pearl could tell something was wrong, the light had gone out of their eyes. When she left she said, "I think something is going on here you don't want me to know. When I leave I'm going to call on the other containers."

The next few days were the worst. It was the beginning of the last week. They hadn't been fed in two days and no one came to clean or restock the pantry. They all went to bed hungry, hoping and praying things would get better. Late that night they were all awakened by the sound of screaming, one of the girls was being raped. The older boys tried to stop the rapist but he wasn't alone. The boys were beaten senseless as the three men took turns on the poor girl. One of the boys managed to make it to the red button and pushed it several time but nothing happened, no one came to help.

The next morning, very early, Pearl appeared in their room. No one was sleeping, not after what had happened the night before but nobody heard the door open. A dim light from a small window in our door softly lit the room.

"I'm so sorry to have to tell you this but all of this is a lie. I just found out last night by spying on my boss. Everything that has happened to you and the others was all planned. They wanted you to be calm for a while, to get your defenses down, to make you think you were all going to be adopted by rich Americans. That was the biggest lie of all. They are going to sell all of you into slavery, to be servants and prostitutes.

"It breaks my heart to have to tell you this, the red button doesn't work, it never worked other than to flash a light in the boss man's quarters. They wanted to see how long it would be before you would try to fight back. The longer you went without pushing the button, the more they were certain you wouldn't resist when you found out the truth.

"I'm so ashamed to have been part of their evil scheme. I will try to get off the ship and contact the police but I think they may be on to me. If they are, I am certain they will kill me."

Those were her final words. They never saw her again.

Somehow, they survived, Jade guessed they wanted to keep all the children alive so they could sell them. They gave them just enough food to keep them from starving to death. Moon got sick a few days before the journey ended. Jade worried so much for her. Every time Moon ate, she vomited everything back up. When Jade touched her face, her sister felt very hot. The last time someone brought them some food they gave Moon some pills but she couldn't swallow them. Jade was so afraid her sister would die. She prayed to God someone would care enough to help poor Moon, to help them all to survive.

CHAPTER 10

The Rescue—Joshua Brown

I pulled my vehicle up to the security gate at Terminal 6, rolled down my window and flashed my creds at the guard. He looked at the creds then shined his flashlight in my face to check if what he saw matched my creds. He looked down at his clipboard, then looked up at me and said, "Sorry sir, You're not on my list."

I let out a long sigh and handed him a copy of my orders and said, "I am fully aware I'm not on your list, son. This is a classified mission as you can plainly see on my orders. Please don't make me late for my appointment. It will not go well for you if I'm late."

The guard quickly scanned my orders then said, "I can let you in sir but someone will have to go with you."

I sighed again and raised my voice to show my frustration, "Son, if someone goes with me, it won't be a confidential operation. Please read the orders again and be quick about it."

I watched him pretend to read my orders then he came to attention and saluted me, "You're cleared to enter, sir."

"Thank you, son," I said as the gate went up and I drove through. I headed towards the five containers and noted the three black SUVs with dark tinted windows parked in front. The container doors were still closed and locked. I counted nine men standing around the SUVs, these men were the muscle waiting for the bosses. I checked my watch and pinned on my badge as I drove up, making sure my body cam was turned on before getting out of my car.

There were nine of them, three from each SUV, all Asian. I introduced myself. "I'm special agent Joshua Brown, all of you are under arrest for participating in the slave trade and numerous other charges. Please put all weapons you may have on the ground and step away from the containers."

They looked at each other then back at me as if they couldn't believe I was that stupid. The biggest, baddest one of the group spit on my boot and said, "No English."

So, I repeated myself in Mandarin and then in Cantonese and waited for them to reply. After a few moments of silence, there was the slightest of nods from the leader and the others slowly began to spread out, drawing weapons that looked like hatchets.

I shook my head, resigned to the violence that was about to happen but I gave it one more try. "Put down your weapons or I will have to use deadly force to stop you," I said in Mandarin.

The leader barked out a command and the two men on the left and right started to throw their hatches at me. I drew both my weapons and shot the hands off the two men, knocking the hatchets into the air, then shot them in the head. It all happened so fast, the other potential hatchet throwers also died within a few seconds of the first. All that remained was the boss.

He showed no sign of remorse for the loss of his men and gave no indication he was giving up. Instead he spit on my other shoe and said in broken English, "You think this over? You think you won something? You are fool. You waste bullets on peasants. Wait until my boss finds out you stole new slaves. You already dead."

I had seen him palm his throwing knife as he rambled on. I let him throw it at me and it was an excellent throw. The blade sunk into the middle of my body armor. I stood perfectly still for a moment to allow him to think he had killed me, then shot him in both his eyes.

I checked my watch, right on time. I left the bodies where they had fallen, got back into my car and drove to where the tour buses were stored. I left my car and picked one of the biggest buses, a bright yellow one, then used my pass key to open the door and start the engine. I was back at the container site in ten minutes.

I used another pass key to open the first container and walked through the narrow opening between tall wooden crates into where the Vietnamese children were housed. I panned my flashlight around the room and counted twenty-eight children, varying in age from around eight to older teenagers. They were all in their bunk beds, eyes opened wide, a look of defeat on each face, terrified I was going turn them into slaves. It broke my heart to see that look of fear.

I spoke to them in Vietnamese. I spoke softly, hoping to gain their trust. "Hello, my name is Joshua. I've come to take you away from the evil men who have been hurting you. I will take you to a place where you will be safe from the evil men. I promise, I will not let you be hurt anymore. Please gather your things and meet me outside."

At first, no one moved but then a young teenage girl said in a soft voice, "Please, sir, can you help my sister, she is very sick. I think she is dying."

I walked over to the teenage girl's bed and saw her younger sister huddled against her. I reached out slowly and placed my hand on the young girl's forehead, she was burning up. "What's your sister's name?"

"She is Moon, I am Jade."

"Jade, is it all right for me to pick Moon up and take her to the bus? She needs to see a doctor as soon as possible."

Jade nodded and handed me her sister's teddy bear.

As gently as I could, I picked her up and started walking slowly towards the exit. Jade followed behind me and I could hear the others getting up and also following. When they got outside, they saw the bodies of the nine evil men I'd killed and stopped walking.

One boy asked, "Who are these dead men?"

I answered, "They're the evil men who were going to make you slaves. They tried to stop me from saving you."

"Did you kill them?" he asked.

"Yes. They tried to kill me and I killed them first."

"Good," said the boy. "They deserved to die."

As we began walking to the bus, the boy spit in the face of one of the evil dead men.

I quickly gathered up the children from the other containers, and got them on the bus. Before leaving, I gave Moon some aspirin with a sip of water.

I drove the few miles from the containers to the same security gate I'd entered. The same guard came out to see what was going on. I slid open the window next to the driver's seat and he asked, "Are you okay sir? I thought I heard gunfire."

"Everything's fine, son. My confidential meeting went well. I'm borrowing this bus. It will be returned in a few days. If anyone asks, you never saw me or heard anything. This mission must remain our secret, understand?"

The guard came to a ridged attention, saluted me and said, "Yes sir. I understand. My lips are sealed."

As we reached Marine Drive and headed into the city of Portland, I noticed a caravan of ten black panel trucks heading towards Terminal 6. I smiled to myself. That was a problem for another day. One day at a time.

CHAPTER 11

Murders at Terminal 6—Detective Hong

The call came in during the middle of the night. A routine check of the container storage area by the terminal's security detail reported the brutal murder of nine Asian men. The massacre (their words not mine) took place in front of five opened containers.

I was on the night shift covering any homicides that took place during the wee small hours of the Portland night. There were three of us and it was my turn to set up the crime scene, notify the criminal investigation unit and make sure the night-shift ME was available.

All of us headed out to the terminal fifteen minutes later. When we arrived at the south security gate, I could see the lit-up crime scene several miles away. Local uniforms had closed off the area with yellow tape and I had the others head for the scene while I questioned the guard.

"Busy night," I said to the guard. "Did you see what went down?"

He shook his head while he looked over at the lit-up area. There were several squad cars and the criminal investigation van, all with their red and blue flashing lights still burning. "No, officer. I didn't see anything."

"Detective," I said. "Officers wear uniforms. I'm a homicide detective."

His head turned back to look at me and he grimaced. "Sorry, I knew that, I guess all those murders have got me upset."

"So, you didn't see anything out of the ordinary? Nothing at all?"

He looked at me with a blank stare for almost a minute before he said, "Well I didn't see anything but I might have heard some gun shots. This place has all kinds of strange noises going on, especially at night. At the time, I didn't think much of it but it could have been gun shots."

"Anything else?"

"No detective, that's all."

I gave him my card and asked him to call me if he thought of anything else. As I drove to the crime scene, I wondered why he was lying to me. I would visit him again, soon.

As I walked under the tape, I realized it really had been a massacre. The nine corpses were spread out and all had hatchets lying close by, except for the ones on the far left and far right. Both of those corpses were also missing their right hands. They had been blown off by some substantial firepower.

The hatchets were the weapons of choice by some of the Tongs, the Chinese equivalent of the Mafia. Maybe this was a battle between two Tong factions, the first round of a turf war? We'd find out soon enough.

There was a throwing knife near the body of the largest of the men. The ME was just finishing up with him as he rolled the corpse over onto his back. "Now there's something you don't see every day," he said.

"What's that?" I asked as I looked over the ME's shoulder. "Oh! You're right. Any powder burns on his face?" I asked, looking at the entry wounds. "That's the first time I've seen a corpse who was shot through both eyes."

The ME answered, "No burns. He was shot from at least ten feet away."

It took another hour to finish the crime scene investigation and to get all the bodies packed up and sent to the police morgue.

The next step was to check out the five containers. They had been converted into living areas for what was assumed to have been slave quarters. It was looking like they were used for human trafficking. The containers had arrived on the dock yesterday and came from the *Kobiashi Maru*. It's last port of call was Singapore.

This just kept getting better and better but my shift was ending and I was beat. I knew my boss was going to call me in tomorrow morning to brief him on what we had so far. It had been a long night and would be a longer day tomorrow.

As I drove back to the city, I kept thinking something was vaguely familiar about how that one man was shot in both eyes. I thought I heard about something like this not too long ago. But that was a problem for another day.

CHAPTER 12

Grace Bible Church—Pastor Bao

I stood on the steps of the church and looked up at the sky. It was a beautiful day with large white, puffy clouds scattered throughout the brilliant blue sky. I took a deep breath and could smell a touch of the morning mist that was so common in Portland after the rain.

I saw the bus coming up the hill. It was a big, bright yellow bus with the words **Port of Portland Terminal 6 Tours** written on the side in big, bold letters. The bus hissed to a stop in the church parking lot and a very large black man stepped out and walked towards me.

I waved at my friend. "Hello, Joshua. It's so good to see you again. I think you have brought me a surprise."

"Hello, Pastor Bao. It shouldn't be a surprise after our meeting yesterday," he replied. He embraced me in a massive bear hug, gentle but massive. "I have brought you nearly a hundred refugees. One little girl, her name is Moon, is very sick. She needs to see a nurse or a doctor as soon as possible. Didn't you mention your lovely wife is a medical person?"

As we walked towards the bus, I answered, "In Vietnam, she was a doctor but unfortunately Oregon doesn't accept her credentials. Let me take a look at the child, then I will call my wife and get our new friends settled."

The child was indeed sick. I called my wife and asked her to join us in the church basement. I told Joshua to move the bus to the rear parking lot where it would be out of sight from the street. As I carried Moon inside the church and took her down the stairs to a small bedroom we used occasionally, I had Joshua bring the other children through the back door and down into the large multipurpose room.

My wife, Cam, joined us with her doctor's bag and shooed me out of the room while she examined Moon. I helped the children get settled. It was obvious they were exhausted and traumatized from all they had been forced to endure for so long. While they rested, I took Joshua aside to discuss logistics.

"How long can they stay in your church?" he asked.

"Actually," I replied, "it's not my church. I am the minister of the Vietnamese Ministry, sort of a church within a church. We hold our services in this basement most of the time. Those of us who also speak English sometimes attend one of the two services in the main sanctuary upstairs. The main church is a non-denominational Christian church, our part of the church is also Christian.

"I haven't as yet spoken to the senior pastor of the church regarding our refugees. Fortunately, he is on vacation until next week. I will discuss it with him when he returns. I cannot guarantee he will let them stay. So, we have at least ten days they can stay here before they may have to leave."

Cam joined us and told us about Moon. "She has a very serious infection. I started her on antibiotics, she'll need to take them for ten days. I think she should be isolated until her fever is gone."

Cam looked at me, then at Joshua and said, "Do you two have a plan on what to do with the children?"

I nodded my head. "Yes my love. Don't I always have a plan? I haven't shared it with Joshua yet. I'm glad you're here so I can tell you both at the same time. Listen closely, my wife and let me know what you think of it. You know how much I value your opinion."

Cam's mouth dropped open and she turned from me to speak to Joshua, "Okay, who is this man and what have you done with my husband?"

It was a good plan. Cam and I would take care of finding homes for the children, freeing up Joshua to take care of his business with the Tong.

CHAPTER 13

The Investigation Continues—Detective Hong

I was driving into headquarters when my phone rang. I punched the button on my dashboard for the hand's-free call, "This is Detective Hong, who's speaking please?"

There was a brief pause followed by, "Uh, Good morning, detective. This is Mark Riley, the security guard at Terminal 6. You said to call you if I thought of anything else that happened last night."

"What did you remember, Mr. Riley?"

"About an hour after I heard the noise that sounded like gun shots, a ten panel-truck caravan came through the security gate. They were on my list of approved visitors so I let them in. I really didn't watch where they were going. My shift was almost over and I was getting ready to sign out."

"Could you ID the driver of the lead truck?"

"No sir, he just lowered the driver side window and showed me his authorization pass for the group. There were no lights in the truck so I couldn't see much but his pass was okay and they were on the list so I raised the gate and let them through."

"It sounds like it was routine."

"It was but they left ten minutes later. They couldn't possibly have loaded ten trucks in that short of time. I just thought you might want to know."

I thanked him for the information and continued my drive to the office. I thought about what he said and the tone of his voice when he said it. He still wasn't giving me the whole story.

When I arrived at headquarters, I parked my car and headed to my desk. My boss was waiting for me. "You're late," he said with a scowl on his face. But he always had a scowl on his face so it was tough to read him.

"Cut me some slack, boss. I was up most of the night covering the murders at Terminal 6."

"You and your partner, in my office now," he growled, turned and headed for his office door.

I looked at my partner, Bill, better known as Buffalo, and checked out his desk. "Where are the donuts?" I asked.

"Chinese people don't like donuts," he answered and headed into the office. I followed him in.

The boss got right to it. "What have you got so far? Hong, you start."

I quickly ran through the events of the previous evening, including the phone call I got this morning from the security guard. When I was done, he was still scowling. "Okay, enough of the facts. What do you think happened?"

"I think the Japanese container ship was part of a human trafficking op. Five containers were removed from the ship earlier in the day and placed together in the container storage area. Late last night, three black SUVs entered Terminal-6 carrying nine Asian men, probably of Chinese descent. They entered the south security gate and stopped at the five containers. They didn't attempt to open the containers. I believe they were security for another group who was to arrive later. The security guard said a caravan of ten panel trucks came through the security gate an hour after the three SUVs. I believe that group was going to pick up the human cargo from the containers and bring them into town but somebody or possibly several somebodies, beat them to it."

"How do you know someone beat them to it?" growled our boss.

"Because the security guard said all the panel trucks left in less than ten minutes. There wouldn't have been enough time for them to drive to the container site, a three-minute drive, unlock the containers, get a hundred slaves loaded up into the trucks and drive another three minutes back to the gate."

"How do you know there were a hundred slaves?" he growled again.

"Because we checked all five containers and each one could accommodate up to thirty people. By the looks of the living areas, most of the beds had been slept in."

"Any IDs on the dead guys?"

"Not yet but we're working on it," answered Buffalo. "We should have more by this afternoon. All we know for sure is they were all Asian, wearing identical black uniforms and carrying metal hatchets"

"Tongs?!!!" We had the boss's full attention now. "Holy crap, don't tell me the Tong are back in town."

Just to brighten my boss's day, I added, "They never really left, they just went underground and diversified."

"Hong don't mess with me. You're back on day shift starting now. I want a full report on the Tong by tonight. This better not be the start of another Tong War. God help us!"

We left the boss and headed to our desks. I did a quick pass by Buffalo as he headed to the restroom. I pulled out his chair and saw the box: a dozen donuts. I took two chocolate cake with chocolate frosting, closed the box and slid his chair under his desk. Nobody hides donuts from me. I can smell them from ten feet away. Chinese have a very keen sense of smell.

After finishing the donuts and washing them down with office coffee, I felt much better. Buffalo Bill saw me eating the last bite and just smiled at me. "I got a call from investigation. They have a copy of the security gate's closed-circuit camera from last night. Do you want to take a look before you check out the Tong scene?"

"Yeah, I don't think my buddy, the security guard, lied to me. He just forgot a few details." I walked around to Bill's desk as he inserted the thumb drive and we began to watch. He cued up the video to begin when the three SUVs had passed through the gate, then fast forward until the next vehicle showed up. It looked like a spinoff of a Humvee. It had government plates but the numbers were obscured and couldn't be read. As best we could tell there was only one occupant in the vehicle but there was no way we could get a good shot of him for a facial recognition ID. There appeared to be a rather lengthy conversation going on between the occupant and the security guard. The guard kept shaking his head and the occupant kept handing him papers to read. Finally, the guard handed back the papers then stepped back, came to attention, saluted the driver and opened the gate.

"Wow!" was all I could think to say. "The driver must have been some high-ranking military person."

We kept watching as a half hour went by with no one entering or leaving. It looked like the guard was getting ready to leave when a very large Terminal-6 tour bus pulled up to the exit gate and waited for the guard to come out. The bus driver slid his side window open as the guard walked around the front of the bus. It didn't look like there was any conversation going on. The guard came to attention, saluted again, lifted the gate and watched the bus leave Terminal-6 heading for Portland.

A few minutes went by and the ten panel trucks approached the entrance and the guard let them enter the yard. Nine minutes and thirty-seven seconds later, all ten panel trucks exited the terminal and headed back to Portland.

We watched as the next shift of security came on duty and Mark Riley left for home.

"We really need to bring that security guard in for questioning," said Bill. "Why don't I take a uniform with me and go pick him up while you get in contact with your Tong friends?"

"Sounds like a plan," I answered. "Can I take the rest of the donuts with me? It's always good to bring a pastry gift when calling on the Tong. You know how much we Chinese love donuts."

Bill just shook his head and chuckled. "While you're down in Chinatown, can you bring me some Moo Goo Gai Pan with a side of collard greens? You know how much us black folk loves Chinese food."

CHAPTER 14

An Eye for an Eye, a Tooth for a Tooth—
Joshua Brown

Before leaving Pastor Bao, I sat down the older children from each of the five containers and showed them pictures of the crew of the *Kobiashi Maru.* I asked them to identify, as best they could, the men who brought the food and cleaned their living space. I also wanted to know which men assaulted them. The children were all very helpful, especially the girls who had been molested or raped.

It took a few hours but I ended up with a list of twenty-three men. All Asian, mostly Japanese, a few spoke Vietnamese.

The *Kobiashi Maru* was due to sail in two days, with only one stop at Longview, Washington, on their way down the Columbia River and back to Singapore. I wanted to make sure I had completed my business with the men before the ship set sail.

The morning after I had brought the children to Grace Bible Church, Cam had woken me and told me some tragic news. They found the body of a young Vietnamese woman floating in the river. She had been raped and beaten severely. Cause of death was a knife wound across her throat.

I took the tour bus back to Terminal 6 and picked up my vehicle. A different security guard at the gate waved me through without having me stop. Apparently, the tour buses picked up passengers in Portland on occasion and it wasn't out the ordinary for a bus to be returning. I parked the bus and walked the half-mile to retrieve my vehicle. I did a quick walk-around before getting in. Nothing was out of place or disturbed, just another visitor parked in the lot. No one stopped me as I drove out the gate and headed back to Portland. I had a few things I had to arrange.

Later that night, I went aboard the *Kobiashi Maru* accompanied by two federal marshals. People may not be aware rivers in the United States don't belong to any of the states they run through. They are all considered federal land and can be policed by federal marshals as well as the FBI.

I had contacted the marshal's office in Portland to assist me in arresting and removing twenty-three of the ship's crew, charging each of them with human trafficking, aggravated assault, rape and murder. I showed the marshal in charge of the Portland office my creds and the arrest warrants, including the pictures of men to be arrested and the complaints made by their victims. I made him aware of the urgency of making the arrests as the ship was to sail the next day.

The captain, accompanied by a representative of the ship's owner, were ashore on personal business and not available. However, the first mate assisted us in taking all twenty-three men from their bunks and isolating them in the crew's mess. As planned, they had all been asleep and somewhat disoriented as I began to question them.

"Good evening gentlemen," I said in Japanese. "Does everyone here speak Japanese?"

Everyone nodded and I continued, "I am Special Agent in Charge, Joshua Brown. You are all being charged with several crimes, including human trafficking, assault and murder."

That got their attention. They jumped up from their seats and began protesting, several attempted to run for the exits but between my marshals and the ship's security personnel, nobody escaped. I gave them a few minutes to calm down. When they were seated I told them the evidence we had against them.

"I know that many of you were just doing what you were told to do. I will dismiss all charges on the first person who tells me who told you to treat the Vietnamese children badly. You can remain on the ship and return to Singapore."

Three of the men jumped up and began yelling a name. The man who yelled first was taken aside and questioned by one of the marshals.

When the accused man was brought in and he saw me and the marshals, he panicked and pulled a gun. Apparently, nobody thought to pat him down for a weapon. He saw the man who had accused him and fired his weapon wounding him. He turned toward me and began to fire but I shot and killed him in self-defense.

Things became very chaotic for the next fifteen minutes. The first thing we did was check everyone for weapons. The next, was restraining all the prisoners with plastic ties. While that was happening, the ship's medic was called in to treat the prisoner for the gun-shot wound. Fortunately, it was a flesh wound and while painful, it wasn't life threatening.

The first mate quickly identified the body of the man I shot. He was new to the crew and had boarded the ship in Singapore. His finger prints were scanned and one of the marshals used his smart phone to transmit his prints to a data base and determined he was wanted on a number of human trafficking charges in Asia. *Ah, the wonders of modern technology.*

While we were waiting for the fingerprint results, I spoke with the first mate and requested he contact the ship's captain and the owner's rep to tell them what was going on. I instructed him to inform them they would be met by federal marshals who would escort them back to the ship as soon as possible.

CHAPTER 15

Tongs—Detective Hong

I left the precinct on the east side of the Willamette River, crossed the Burnside Bridge and turned north on 4th Avenue. The Chinatown Gateway spanned the street leading to Chinatown. I pulled over to the side of the street to admire the gate. When it was built in 1986 it was the largest gate of its kind, costing over $250,000. A few months later, a larger one was built in Washington DC. It's still impressive to me and every time I come to visit Uncle Chen I always stop for a few minutes just to see the gate. It brings back fond memories of seeing it for the first time when I was a child. I couldn't take my eyes off it as my parents and I walked down 4th Avenue to have dinner at Chen's Good Taste Restaurant.

Enough nostalgia. The restaurant was just a short distance north of the gate and I pulled my car into the small parking lot and checked my watch, it was just a couple of minutes past 10:00am. I looked up in time to see the neon Open sign flash on with large bright letters, followed by the distinct click of the front door being unlocked.

Two people had been ahead of me and I let them enter before I stepped in. The dining area was dark, they'd discontinued dining-in when the Corona virus hit and never opened up the dining area after it had subsided. Uncle Chen said he saved lots of money by selling only takeout. "No servers to pay, lower electric bills. I make fifty percent more money now," he told me during one of my visits.

Even though the dining area was dark (saving money on no florescent lighting) there was one small lamp over Uncle's favorite booth. Mei Mei, the lone hostess who took phone orders and walk-ins, collected the money or credit cards and gave the customers their food, turned and shouted at Uncle, "Your nephew is here."

"Which one? I have so many nephews," he shouted back.

"Your favorite one," she yelled and turned back to take an order.

"Nephew Hong, indeed you are my favorite nephew. I am so glad you have come to visit me. What gift did you bring me?" he said in Mandarin.

I didn't lift up the box of donuts for him to see as I walked toward his booth. Uncle was nearly blind. I was almost to his table when he said, "Donuts, you brought me donuts. How kind of you." He turned and shouted in the general direction of the hostess, "Mei Mei, a fresh pot of tea for me and my favorite nephew."

He may not be able to see very well but his sense of smell was strong. I stopped at the table and bowed deeply. He nodded his head and smiled as I placed the box on the table and sat down opposite him.

First the pleasantries. It isn't polite in the Chinese culture to speak of business without the pleasantries and they always come first. "How are you Uncle Chen? I see your take out business is doing well."

"I can't complain except for the lazy cooks. If they would only work a little faster I could make more money. How have you been, favorite nephew Hong? It's been several weeks since I saw you last. I was concerned something had happened to you."

"I am fine Uncle. I should have informed you I was assigned to the night-shift two weeks ago. I am back on days now and will see you more often. My partner, Buffalo Bill, sends his regards and said not to come back to work without an order of your famous Moo Goo Gai Pan."

"I like your partner. He is very polite to me when you two come to my humble restaurant. He is married, is he not?"

I nodded, knowing what was coming next.

"Have you found any worthy woman whom you would consider marrying? You are in your prime. Many Chinese women find you attractive and would jump at the chance to be your bride."

I smiled at him and said, "As a matter of fact, I am seeing a woman. Her name is Lili."

"A Chinese girl?" he asked excitedly.

"Yes," I answered. "She's a beautiful Chinese girl." I took my phone and showed him a picture of Lili.

"You're correct. She is very beautiful. Is she Chinese or ABC?"

I paused before answering. I needed to phrase my reply carefully. "Lili is first generation American Born Chinese. She speaks both Mandarin and Cantonese fluently. Her mother has raised her to value the ways of the Chinese culture."

Uncle sat silently for a moment, then I noticed a slight smile on his face. "I would very much like to meet this Lili. I can tell you have deep feelings for her. At least she isn't a *gweilo.*"

He turned and shouted to Mei Mei, "One order of Moo Goo Gai Pan to go for my favorite nephew's partner."

The pleasantries were over. It was time to get down to business.

I asked Uncle, "I'm sure you're aware that nine Chinese hatchet men were killed yesterday at Terminal 6. I'm trying to find out which Tong they are from and who killed them. My boss is concerned it was another local Tong or perhaps some new talent from out of state."

Uncle sipped his tea and munched on a plain cake donut as I asked my question. He finished the donut and reached for another, a glazed with strawberry frosting this time. "Yes, I am aware. I believe it was a local Tong who decided to make money in human trafficking Asian children. They explained to the council their normal source of funding had recently dried up. They were acting as a go-between for those who collect the children and those who would turn them into slaves or prostitutes. The council ruled against them but they were committed for at least one attempt at making it work."

"Can you tell me the name of the Tong?" I asked.

"No, I am bound by the code of the council not to reveal the name of any Tong involved with illegal activities. However, I believe a veteran detective like yourself can discover which Tong has lost nine of their soldiers in one night."

"Who do you think killed the Tong's men?" I asked as I watched him finish his second donut, licking the frosting off his fingers.

He took a sip of tea and dried his fingers with a napkin, then said, "I don't know who killed the Tong but I know it wasn't anyone local. I believe it was just one man who killed all nine. A very formidable man to kill nine well trained soldiers. Please be careful, my favorite nephew. I look forward to meeting your new girlfriend soon. Ah, here is Mei Mei with the takeout for your partner. No charge today. Thank you for your gift of a dozen donuts minus two. See you soon."

I stood, bowed and left the restaurant, picking up a copy of today's Chinese language newspaper on my way out.

I made it to my car just before it started to rain. I began thumbing through the pages of the newspaper as the rain beat down on the roof of my car until I came to the obituaries. Tongs are very close-knit groups, usually composed of family members. That can include very distant relatives or even friends of relatives. A Tong family takes care of each of their members. When one of them dies, they usually print the name of the deceased and the name of the Tong he belongs to in the Chinese newspaper. It would be very unusual for a Tong to lose nine members in a single day.

It took only a few minutes to find what I was looking for, The name of nine men who lost their lives yesterday. They were all from the same Tong, The Bing Hop Tong. I decided to have a chat with the leader of Bing Hop.

I started the car, turned on the windshield wipers and drove the three blocks to their office. As I pulled into their parking area, the first thing I noticed were several black panel trucks, just like the ones Bill and I had seen on the Terminal-6 security footage. I took a few pictures to compare with the footage. I also got a few license plate numbers.

I pulled into a vacant spot and saw a flurry of activity. People were loading computers, data storage devices and a lot of office stuff into the remaining panel trucks. I grabbed my umbrella, stepped out of the car and stopped the first person I saw. I showed him my creds. "I need to see your leader," I said.

The man looked at my creds, then looked up at me. "You're too late. He was murdered an hour ago, along with six others of our ruling council. There are police in the building over there." He gestured with his head as he loaded more stuff into the van.

I headed over to the building to check on what had happened. I met Bill coming down the stairs from the second floor. "Hey partner. It's about time. Didn't you get my text?"

"No, I turned it off while I was with Uncle Chen," I answered. "What have you got?"

"It's a real blood bath upstairs. It looks like the Tong leadership was trying to bug out but somebody got to them first. Survivors are few but they said it was a group of four men with automatic weapons who never said a word. They just walked in and started shooting. I guess they were upset they didn't get their slaves delivered to them."

"Did you get anything on the shooters?" I asked.

"Nada," he replied. "Just one thing the three survivors agreed on, they weren't Asian. We got confirmation from a couple of the Bing Hop people who were loading the panel trucks. A black SUV pulled in and four men with automatic weapons ran into the building, quickly killed the leaders, ran back to the SUV and burned rubber leaving. It couldn't have been more than a few minutes tops. They wore ski masks, but they were all white *gweilos.*"

We both headed back to the precinct. As soon as we arrived we started looking at traffic camera footage of the area. It took us about thirty minutes to identify the SUV leaving the scene. Then another fifteen minutes to follow them on a series of traffic cams to a warehouse where they dumped the SUV and left in four different directions on foot. A few minutes later we lost contact with them.

I was frustrated. It seemed like every one of the bad guys were just a step ahead of us. We have no idea who killed the Tong soldiers at Terminal 6 but we're pretty certain it was a lone shooter. I got a lead from my uncle which Tong family the dead soldiers were from and by some brilliant detective work, I deduced it was the Bing Hop. I went to the Bing Hop headquarters and found out the Tong leaders were killed just before I got there. They were killed by *gweilos* with machine guns who seemed to disappear into thin air. Oh, by the way, a *gweilo* is anyone who isn't Chinese. It can be used for other Asian races but most often for non-Asians. It has a number of meanings. Most *gweilos* believe it means 'foreigner' but when said by a Chinese person with a lot of gusto, it means 'round eyed devil.'

"So, where do we go from here?" I turned to Buffalo Bill and asked, "How did the interrogation of the Terminal 6 security guard go? I hope you got something out of him we can use."

"Nope," he answered. "I was on my way to pick him up but got diverted to cover the Bing Hop headquarter murders. By the way, did you get my Moo Goo Gai Pan?"

I placed the bag on his desk. "You may want to nuke it a bit. It's probably cold by now."

"Where are the rest of the donuts?" he asked as he picked up the bag and headed for the break room. I followed him in and sat at one of the tables and watched him place his food in the microwave.

"Uncle kept them," I replied. "He loves donuts more than I do. I told you I was going to give them to him as a gift."

As the microwave counted down, Buffalo Bill turned to face me. "You lyin' to me. You ate 'um all yourself. You'd da best donut hound I knows."

"I love it when you talk all southern. Stop complaining. Uncle gave me your meal for free. He gave me a hard time when he found out there were only ten in the box. I told him you ate them."

The microwave dinged and Buffalo Bill took the steaming plate of Chinese food and sat down at the table. "Share that with me, I haven't had anything to eat all day except those two donuts this morning," I said in my most whiny voice.

Buffalo Bill looked up and smiled as he encircled his plate with his arm and began smacking his lips as he ate. "This is too good to share. Next time get your own."

CHAPTER 16

Pursuit of the *Gweilos*—Joshua

I had just pulled up on my bike across the street from the Bing Hop headquarters building when I heard the gun fire. I also heard screaming and then nothing. A few minutes later, I heard the closing of four car doors, an engine roaring to life and the screech of tires. The SUV shot out of the parking lot next to the building, tires squealing as it turned sharply to miss oncoming traffic then accelerating quickly toward the warehouse district. I started my bike and followed.

They were coming up on a busy intersection and the light was red. I was mildly surprised to see red and blue lights flashing on the SUV and a brief blip of a siren. They never slowed as they barreled through the red light. The crossing traffic had ground to a halt and I managed to get through before they recovered. Three blocks in they made a fast turn and drove through the open door of a warehouse. The door immediately closed behind the SUV and I coasted up to a location where I could see two sides of the building and waited. A few seconds later, four men dressed in black combat gear came running out of a side door and into an alley, shedding their gear as they ran. By the time they made it to the street they separated and began walking in different directions at a leisurely pace. I picked one and began to follow him, maintaining a healthy distance behind him. He walked for about fifteen minutes, reversing his course several times and crossing back and forth across the street checking to see if he was being followed. He was a pro and had all the skills. But I had skills of my own. I was dressed in regular civilian clothes and acting like a tourist.

We were still in the Chinatown area and there were lots of things to see and photograph. When he made one of his reversals I kept walking toward him. Immediately behind him was the Chinatown Gate and several people were taking pictures. I grabbed my phone, set it to camera mode and clicked off several shots, including one with my subject dead center.

As he passed me, I headed for the corner and crossed the street to the other side and continued to follow him. As I walked, I threw away my hat and took off my jacket and gave it to a homeless man begging on the street. When I turned to walk away, I began to walk with a pronounced limp.

A few minutes later, I saw the other three men standing outside a Chinese restaurant pretending to read the menu posted on the wall next to the opened front door. My subject headed directly toward them. I was behind him and slipped off my shirt but kept on my Phoenix Suns T-shirt. I slipped on a pair of sunglasses and stopped limping as I closed the gap between us. I stood next to him at the intersection while we waited for the light to change. The other three were across the street pretending they didn't see him.

Just as the light changed and we began to walk across the street, a blue Nissan Murano pulled up to the curb and stopped, the side doors opened wide. The three men quickly got in and my suspect turned left and followed them in. I was momentarily out of sight and attached a tracker under the vehicle's bumper as I pretended to tie my shoe. The next second, they were gone.

I stood up and watched them as they drove away. I took my phone and sent the suspect's picture to the photo recognition software app. Then I turned and walked back to my ride. I knew the police were probably in the warehouse now and setting up a crime scene. As I walked down the alley to my bike, I spotted the yellow tape and crime scene investigation van. I got on my bike, fired it up and left the scene. When I got to my destination, I checked the phone. I smiled. Now I knew who my suspect was. It was just a matter of time until I had him and his buddies in custody. If everything went well, there was a good chance I'd be able to determine who they were working for.

CHAPTER 17

The Interview/Interrogation—Detective Hong

The next morning, Buffalo Bill and I drove to the home of Mark Riley, the Terminal 6 security guard who was on duty the night of the murders. We called to make sure he was at his apartment. He answered on the third ring. "This is Mark, who's calling please?"

"Good morning, Mark," I replied. "This is detective Hong. I'm calling to see if you're available for me and my partner to ask you a few questions." There was a long pause. "Hello, are you still there?"

"Yes, sorry. I had to let my dog outside. What type of questions? Am I in trouble?"

"Not at all," I answered. "This is just a routine follow-up. We're hoping you might have thought of more details of what happened the night of the murders."

Another pause, then he answered, "Okay, sure. I'll be home for at least a couple of hours."

He gave us his address and we drove to his apartment in the Woodlawn district in northeast Portland. When we arrived, the light drizzle had stopped. His apartment was on the first floor and had a small, fenced in patio area. When we knocked on his door we could hear the barking of his dog. From the sound of it, he was a big dog.

The door opened, and Mark invited us inside. I introduced him to Bill (only his friends called him Buffalo Bill). He was dressed in a pair of shorts and a tank top revealing a strong, athletic body. By his bearing, I thought he must have been in the military.

His apartment was a small, two-bedroom unit, definitely a man-cave. He invited us to sit at his table in the kitchen nook and asked us if we would like some coffee or water. We thanked him but declined. His dog hadn't stopped barking since we knocked on the door.

I was about to begin with the questions when Mark asked, "Excuse me. Would you mind if I brought my dog in so he could get your scent and to see you aren't a threat to me? It won't take more than a few minutes. If I don't do that, he will continue to bark as long as you are here."

I looked at Bill, he nodded. I said, "Sure, go ahead."

Mark got up and opened the door to the patio and in walked the biggest German Shepherd I had ever seen. He had stopped barking but he looked at Buffalo Bill and me as if we were fresh meat. I was beginning to wish I hadn't agreed to letting the dog in.

"Front!" said Mark and the dog moved to his right side. "Sit, Sergeant" The dog sat but never took his eyes off of us. "I'm going to have him check you out, one at a time. Sarge, approach."

Sarge stood and approached me first. He walked up to me sniffing me all over. Then he surprised me by, jumping up and placing his paws on my leg. I froze as he looked me in the eyes, waiting for reaction on my part. Mark said, "Slowly pet him on the head."

I reached over with my left hand (I wanted to protect my gun hand) and pet the beast. His eyes seemed to soften as he left me and went over to Buffalo Bill. The dog went through the same routine, except when Bill petted him, he also scratched his ears and said, "You're a good dog, Sarge." The dog quickly looked at Mark who nodded. The dog began wagging his tail and licking Bill on the cheek.

Mark called to the dog, "Front." Sarge left Bill and returned to Mark who handed him a treat and sent him outside. He never barked once while we questioned Mark.

"So, I assume you were a dog handler in the military?"

"That's correct, detective. We served two tours in Afghanistan. I was Sarge's handler. Our assignment was to discover

IEDs so they could be disarmed. We were both wounded three days before the end of our second tour. We both were awarded purple hearts and retired from active duty with the corps."

"Thank you for your service, thank Sarge too." Said Bill. "That is one fine Marine."

Mark smiled at the compliment, then his expression sobered. "I guess I left out some details about what happened the night of the murders but I was under orders."

That got our attention. "Whose orders?" I asked.

"I'm sure you've seen the security video from the south gate. The man who arrived at the gate the night of the murders was a former officer, a high-ranking officer. He was on a classified assignment from our government. I was instructed by him not to lie to the police but not to reveal any details about him until instructed to do so. Last night he contacted me and authorized me to tell you everything that I know about that night with one exception, I'm not to reveal anything about him or his overall mission. He said he would contact you when the time was right."

Wow! That's a stunner. Bill looked at me and I saw the same stunned expression on his face that was on mine. I looked back at Mark and said, "Tell us everything you know about that night."

For the next hour, Mark unloaded all the details of what happened at the security gate. We asked him to expand on certain items and he was most helpful. But he was true to his word, he told us nothing about the man who gave him his orders.

On the drive back to the precinct, we were quietly going over what Mark had said. Buffalo Bill was the first to speak. "Were going to check out his claim to be in the Marines, aren't we?"

"Of course," I answered. "We have to verify everything he said and compare it to what we already know."

Out of the blue, Bill said, "I really liked Sarge. That was one fine dog."

"You're right. He sure took a liking to you, licking your face and wagging his tail. But you have a special appeal to dogs."

He turned to look at me and said, "How do you know I like dogs? I never recall talking to you about that."

"No, you never did. But you didn't have to. I've seen the girls you date."

We drove on in silence for a few minutes, then Buffalo Bill leaned over and punched me in the arm and said two words. "You asshole."

When we got back to the precinct, we began the process of verifying what Mark had said. Everything he told us about his tours in Afghanistan was spot on, except he had not mentioned he had been awarded a silver star for coming up with a way to remotely detonate IEDs. We read the commendation that justified the award. It reported: During his downtime he built and used micro drones, very inexpensive micro drones, armed with a special laser and microwave antenna that could detect and destroy IEDs from over a hundred yards. The commendation went on to say: Master Sergeant Riley's ingenuity in creating and demonstrating the feasibility of this new defensive weapon will result in saving the lives of hundreds of military personnel and civilians. Additionally, it will prevent the maiming of thousands of individuals occupying combat zones.

Shortly after we'd finished, the boss called us into his office for debriefing of our meeting with Mark. Buffalo Bill told him what we knew and I told him what we thought had happened. I left out Bill's affection for dogs, both the two and four-legged variety.

"Okay boss, here's what we think happened," I said. "About a hundred young men and women, some of them children, were smuggled into Portland against their will. Most of them were Vietnamese. They were brought in on a Japanese container ship form Singapore. Five containers were placed in the container storage yard at Terminal 6. Late that night, members of the Bing Hop

Tong were supposed to pick up the people from the containers and distribute them to as yet unknown dealers in human trafficking. They sent nine of their soldiers to make sure the containers were intact. That was to be followed by other Bing Hop people who would then collect the captives and deliver them to the buyers. We think Bing Hop had negotiated in advance or at least a partial payment.

"It appears, federal agents were aware of this operation and stepped into to nip it in the bud. As difficult as this is to believe, we think one federal agent killed all nine of the Bing Hop soldiers. It may have been in self-defense or just an outright massacre. We don't have enough evidence to be sure which way it went. The fed then opened the five containers and collected all the captives and took them out of Terminal 6 in a tour bus he borrowed."

"What do you mean the fed borrowed the bus?" interrupted the boss.

Bill answered, "The bus was returned the next morning. The buses come and go all day long and nobody gives them much attention. No one noticed who was driving that particular bus. It just showed up in the bus lot. There were no prints on the steering wheel or anywhere else the driver sat."

"Do you know where the fed took the captives?"

"No sir, we don't," I answered.

The boss motioned for me to continue.

"Shortly after the tour bus left with the hostages, a group of ten Bing Hop vans entered the south security gate, presumably to pick up the captives and deliver them to the buyers. At the present time, we're interrogating a surviving Bing Hop driver of one of the vans to see if we can get any information on where they were supposed to deliver the captives."

"Only one driver? What happened to the other nine?" the boss interrupted again.

"Several of the drivers were killed in the raid on Bing Hop headquarters, a few others escaped the scene before the police arrived. Only one remained."

The boss gestured again for us to continue, since Bill was the first detective on the scene, he took over. "A little after 9:00am yesterday morning, a black SUV pulled into the headquarters' parking lot with four masked men wearing combat gear and carrying assault weapons. They ran into the building and shot and killed all of the Tong leadership. They immediately ran back to their vehicle and drove away. The entire attack lasted less than five minutes. We think the killers were hired by whoever paid the Tong to deliver the captives."

"Do we have anything on where the killers might be?" the boss asked.

"Using traffic cam footage we were able to track them to a warehouse a few blocks away from the Bing Hop building. They abandoned the SUV inside the warehouse and left on foot in four different directions. We used various local security cams to follow them but we soon lost track of them."

"I don't suppose you got any pictures of their faces?" the boss growled.

"No sir," Bill answered, "They were all wearing baseball caps pulled low to cover their faces."

The boss sat fuming at his desk for a moment, then scowled at us and asked, "Do you have any good news? Anything at all?"

"Possibly," I answered. "The fed told Mark, the security guard, he was going to contact us with detailed information."

"When will that happen?" growled the boss.

"Sometime soon, we hope," I replied. "In the meantime, we'll work on the Tong van driver to see where the Tong were supposed to deliver the captives."

CHAPTER 18

The Letter to the Portland Police—Joshua Brown

This letter is intended for Detectives Hong and Buffalo Bill. My name is Joshua Brown. I am a field operative of a top-secret organization that very few people know exists. My overall mission objectives are described in a very lengthy document. Basically, I am assigned missions that involve very bad people hurting very humble, God fearing people who cannot protect themselves. My job is to make sure the bad people don't win.

I'll share with you what I can about what happened at Terminal 6. A group of a hundred young people from excruciatingly poor families in Vietnam were told by human traffickers they would buy their children and provide them with rich adoptive parents. Of course, that was a lie. They gave the parents a few dollars and took the children to Ho Chi Min City where they were put on a boat to Singapore. In Singapore they were placed in five shipping containers and loaded on a container ship to Portland at Terminal 6. For most of the young people, their standard of living was greatly improved but only temporarily. By the time they arrived at Terminal 6, they had been starved, beaten and some of the girls raped. One Vietnamese woman tried to protect them and she was beaten, raped and killed for trying to prevent the sale of the young people into slavery and prostitution.

Their containers were taken off the ship and placed in the Terminal 6 container storage yard. The captives were to be taken by members of the Bing Hop Tong and delivered to customers somewhere in the United States. That's where I stepped in. The organization I belong to has an incredibly sophisticated data collection arm. They discovered the ship being used for human trafficking, where and when it would dock and gave me suggestions on how to ensure the captives wouldn't be placed into any further danger.

I arrived at the five containers and confronted the nine Tong soldiers. I told them I was a federal agent and they were all under arrest as accessories to human trafficking, rape and murder. I told them to drop any weapons they might have. They declined my arrest and instead attacked me. I was able to successfully defend myself. All of this is recorded on my body cam and available to you on the thumb drive enclosed with this letter.

Before the Tong reserves showed up to take the captives away, I gathered them all and took them to a safe place. I will not share what happened to them except to say the promises that were made to them in Asia, will be fulfilled here in America.

I attempted to visit the Bing Hop headquarters in Chinatown, only to arrive after the leaders had been brutally murdered. I was able to follow the killers and ascertain where they are now located. They are scheduled to fly out of Portland for Memphis, Tennessee, tomorrow. Airline flight information and the aliases they're traveling under is also supplied in an attachment to this letter as well as the address of their current location. I sincerely hope you will be able to arrest them and keep them from returning to their bosses. These men are extremely dangerous. They will not hesitate to murder anyone who attempts to detain them. I strongly recommend you approach them with your best SWAT team.

There shouldn't be any further human trafficking events using the container ships but you never know. Be vigilant. I will continue to find out who is behind these heinous crimes but since this is no longer a Portland PD problem, I probably won't be in contact with you again. Good hunting gentlemen and God bless.

CHAPTER 19

Save All the Children-Pastor Bao

It was late afternoon. Cam and I were relaxing for a few minutes after our lunch before returning to our work. Cam had prepared my favorite lunch, bun cha. I especially liked the marinated pork bellies, very delicious as were all of the other plates that went with it. Besides being a great cook and an excellent doctor, she is still that beautiful woman I married so many years ago in Saigon.

We were discussing our plans for the Vietnamese children Joshua had left with us. I asked her, "How are the flyers coming for this Sunday's service? Have we received them from the print shop?"

Cam smiled and answered, "The English version or the Vietnamese version?"

Since our senior pastor was still away on vacation, I would be preaching the first two services in English in the main sanctuary, then follow with the same version of the sermon in Vietnamese in our basement multipurpose area. "Both versions. I've been so busy preparing the sermons, I haven't had the chance to review the bulletins."

I paused for a second, then added, "I'm sure you have done your usual outstanding job of preparing both bulletins, getting them printed and picking them up from the printer. What I really want to see is the insert about our Vietnamese guests. Also, I'm concerned if we're doing the right thing including an English version of the insert."

Cam was silent for a moment. I assumed she was determining the best way to tell me what she considered was bad news. She said in a soft voice, "I share your concern, my husband. I know we originally thought to include all the church in our hope of finding enough homes for all the children. It would be doubtful we would find enough of our Vietnamese families willing to take a hundred children. We know not all of the upstairs church members were in favor of having a Vietnamese ministry as part of Grace Bible Church. If we announce our plans to the entire church, I believe there is a good chance someone would go the authorities and all the children could be sent back to the poverty of their homes in Vietnam. Remember, we made a promise to Joshua we would find homes for them all."

She paused, waiting for me to consider what she'd said and my decision how to move forward. Some may think of this as being manipulative, I choose to believe she is being considerate.

"You're correct, my wife. We will not put the English flyers about the children in the upstairs bulletins. We will focus on our Vietnamese community. I'm sure they will understand the delicacy of what we are proposing when we explain it to them," I replied. Then, an idea occurred to me, perhaps an inspiration from God. "What about calling our church families and have them invite other Vietnamese friends who don't attend our church, especially those who have shown an interest in a larger family."

Cam let out a squeal of delight, clapping her hands together. She stood up abruptly and rushed over to me and kissed me on my forehead. I pulled her onto my lap and said, "I take it you like my idea?"

She kissed my forehead a second time and answered, "It's a very good idea, my ever so smart husband. I will begin calling right away." She stood up and started to walk to her office, then turned and added, "The Vietnamese Women's group has a Bible study tomorrow evening. We always have a large group of our ladies attend. How about I brief them before the meeting about what we will be doing on Sunday and encourage them to invite their non-church going friends?"

Now it was my turn. I jumped up and ran to her, grabbing her around her waist and attempting to kiss her on the forehead.

Unfortunately, she is taller than me and I had to settle for kissing her on her mouth. It turned out that wasn't a bad second choice. "A brilliant idea my love," I said as I nuzzled her ear, thinking this was becoming a very pleasant afternoon.

"Not now, lover boy. I have a lot of phone calls to make," she said as she removed my arms from around her waist and turned toward her office. As she walked, she turned her head toward me and said with a coy little smile, "Maybe later, my darling husband."

While Cam was busy making calls, I found the business card that Joshua had given me. It was for an attorney he said was very good, especially when it came to adoptions. The card was printed: **Pham Bin Minh, Attorney at Law specializing in adoptions.** I went online and Googled his web site. The site showed fourteen referrals, all of them tens. Assuming they didn't come from relatives, that was very impressive. I called the number on the card and set up an appointment for the next day.

It turns out the attorney's office was only a short distance from the church. It was in a complex of other small office buildings. I found the building directory and noticed there were several other attorneys listed, about half had Vietnamese names. I found the suite number and entered Mr. Pham's suite into a small lobby. A man in his early thirties was leaning against his office door jamb as I walked into the lobby. He was wearing dark slacks and a white dress shirt with the sleeves rolled up to his elbows. He was surprisingly muscular with short cut hair. He was smiling as he said, "You must be Pastor Bao. I'm Pham Bin Minh. You're right on time. Come on into my office. Can I get you anything, water or coffee?"

He gestured to a chair and I sat down. "No thank you," I replied as I looked around his office. It was very neat, no loose papers on his desk, several bookshelves held numerous legal books and a credenza with three pictures on top. He sat behind his desk and noticed I was looking at his pictures. One was him in a weight lifting suit with a barbell held over his head loaded with so many plates the bar was bending. The second was him in his Marine dress uniform with sergeant strips on his sleeve. The last was him in combat gear standing next to Joshua Brown also dressed in combat gear.

When I turned back to look at him, he said, "Yes, I served with Master Sergeant Brown in Afghanistan. We're very close friends. He told me about your situation and I want you to know, I'm confident we can get the children adopted quickly, as soon as they have been selected by their new families."

I was skeptical. "I thought adoption took years before it became finalized."

He smiled and nodded his head. "In many cases that is true but not in this case. Are you aware that Joshua works for a very…I guess special organization would be the best way to describe it?"

"No, not really," I answered. "I only met with him for a short time. He didn't give me any details of how he came to have a hundred Vietnamese children. He only said they needed to be adopted as soon as possible so they could remain in America. Just looking at them, I could see they had been abused, badly abused. I promised him I would do everything I could to find homes for all of them."

"That sounds like Joshua," said Pham. "He tells you what you need to know to get the job done and not much else. You're going to have to trust me when I say I can get this done quickly. The people Joshua works for can cut through any barriers, like a hot knife through a cube of cold butter. He gave me the names of all the children and short backgrounds on each one. I think I have everything I need to proceed. When do you plan on matching the children with the adoptive parents?"

"This coming Sunday afternoon. Is that too soon?" I asked. Then said, "By the way, do you speak Vietnamese? None of the children speak English and many of our families speak only a little English."

"Sorry," he said in Vietnamese. "I should have been speaking Vietnamese all this time. I was born in Saigon and immigrated to the U.S. when I was twelve. My parents never did learn to speak English. We spoke Vietnamese at home."

"I have one more question," I said, "We're concerned that some of the children will not be selected by members of our congregation. Is there a limit on how many children my wife and I can adopt? I promised Joshua every child would be adopted."

CHAPTER 20

Women's Bible Study Class—Cam Boa

This was going to be a special night. I had called every woman who attended our regular Vietnamese services. I explained this Wednesday's class would be different. I told them about the children and everything they had gone through and how we were hoping to find good families willing to adopt one or two of the children. Seventy-seven said they would attend. Some said they wanted to bring their husbands. I agreed.

On Wednesday morning, I spoke to the children about meeting with the potential new families. Most were enthusiastic. All had believed from the start they were going to be adopted by rich American families. Of course, that was a lie told by evil men. None of us were rich by American standards but after hearing the stories of the poverty they had endured, I was sure they thought all Americans were rich.

There were a few children who were frightened about meeting our families. The few days they had stayed with us at the church was surely a reprieve from what they had suffered in the containers. But the trauma they lived through had lasting effects. I prayed they wouldn't be too upset at meeting new people.

The ladies and a few of the husbands began showing up at 5:30pm to help set up. Tables were set out with snacks and two punch bowls filled with orange and strawberry punch. By 6:00pm the ten tables were filled and additional tables had to be brought in to accommodate everyone. By 6:15pm it was standing room only.

I estimated there were close to two hundred people in the church's large multipurpose room. The children were waiting in a number of rooms on the side of the basement, all dressed in donated clothes from our church people.

It was time to begin. My husband walked out of his office and made his opening comments.

"Ladies and Gentleman, welcome to a very special Wednesday night Bible study class. Tonight, we are going to give you the opportunity to meet some very special people. A few months ago, these young people were living in poverty in Vietnam. Many days they had nothing to eat. Then some ruthless men convinced their parents to sell them for almost nothing, telling them the children were to be adopted by rich Vietnamese families. That was a lie. They ended up in Singapore and told they would be shipped to America and be adopted by rich American families. That was also a lie. It took three weeks to cross the ocean and ended up in Portland to be sold into slavery by human traffickers."

He paused to let that sink in, then continued. "Fortunately, someone rescued the young people from the evil men and brought them to our church. They can't return to the poverty of Vietnam and they can't stay in America unless we can find homes for them. We are asking you to consider adopting one or two of the young people. They don't speak English, only Vietnamese. We are their only hope to live a normal life.

"Tonight, we will introduce you to all of them. They range in age from eight to fifteen. Take the time to speak with them and get to know them. If you find it in your heart to help these young people, I am sure you will be blessed.

"This Sunday, following the Vietnamese service, you will have the opportunity to decide if you want to adopt one or more of these young people. We will have an attorney present who assures me we can complete all adoptions on Sunday before you return to your homes.

"Without further comments from me, let me introduce you to your future children."

During the next two hours the young people mingled with the adults. Everyone seemed to be enjoying the experience. At first, the young people were a little standoffish. But eventually, they warmed up to the adults and seemed to enjoy the attention immensely. They actually began smiling and laughing by the end of the evening. After everyone left and the young people went back to their quarters, I asked my husband what he thought.

"Do you think there is a chance we can find homes for all of them?" I asked.

He thought for a long moment, then answered, "Unfortunately, no. I think many of the younger ones will be adopted. They seemed to be a big hit with everyone. But I'm not so sure about the older ones. We shall see this coming Sunday."

CHAPTER 21

The Good Samaritan-Pastor Boa

I sat in the front pew of the first Sunday service. The choir sang two hymns and one of the elders read a verse from scripture. Another elder had the congregation kneel for prayer, then it was my turn. I stepped up to the pulpit and looked out at all the faces of the congregation, then began. "It's so nice to see you all here this morning. Fortunately for both you and I, Pastor Jacobs will be back in the pulpit preaching next Sunday. I want to thank you all for putting up with me these last two weeks.

"Today, our sermon will be about the Good Samaritan, a parable taught by our Savior Jesus Christ. Please take your Bibles and turn to Luke, chapter ten, beginning in verse twenty-five.

"And behold, a lawyer stood up to put him to the test saying, 'Teacher, what shall I do to inherit eternal life?' He said to him, 'What is written in the Law? How do you read it?' And he answered, 'You shall love the Lord your God with all your heart and with all your soul and with all your strength and with all your mind, and your neighbor as yourself.' And he said to him, 'You have answered correctly, do this and you will live.'

"But he, desiring to justify himself, said to Jesus, 'And who is my neighbor?' Jesus replied, 'A man was going down from Jerusalem to Jericho and he fell among robbers, who stripped him and beat him and departed, leaving him half dead. Now by chance a priest was going down that road and when he saw him, passed on the other side. So likewise a Levite, when he came to the place and saw him, passed by on the other side. But a Samaritan, as he journeyed, came to where he was and when he saw him, he had compassion. He went to him and bound up his wounds, pouring on oil and wine. Then set him on his own animal and brought him to an inn and took care of him. The next day he took out two denarii and gave them to the innkeeper, saying, 'Take care of him and whatever you spend, I will repay you when I come back.' Which of these three, do you think, proved to be a neighbor to the man who fell among the robbers?' He said, 'The one who showed him mercy.' And Jesus said to him, 'You go and do likewise.'"

I closed the Bible, adding, "May our Lord add his blessing to the reading of his word." I looked out at the congregation and said, "Let me add some context to this parable. The man who was beaten by robbers was from Jerusalem, located in Judea. The priest and the Levite were also from Judea. Neither of these two men offered any help to a brother Judean. They would rather have let him die than risk becoming unclean. When they saw him bloody and battered in the middle of the road, they got as far away from him as possible and walked by on the side of the road. Then along comes a Samaritan man.

"Samaritans and Judeans considered each other enemies. When King Solomon died, his kingdom was split into two separate countries, Judea in the south and Israel in the north. The northern kingdom abandoned their belief in God, they became pagans worshiping idols and sacrificing their first-born children to the false god, Baal. Jerusalem had been the capitol of the unified kingdom. It was where the temple of God was built by Solomon. When the kingdom was divided, the northern kingdom built their own capitol, called Samaria and the people who lived in the northern country were referred to as Samaritans.

"To put it bluntly, the Judeans and Samaritans hated each other with a passion. And yet, when the Samaritan saw the man beaten and bloody lying on the road, he didn't hesitate. He didn't know anything about the injured man, he just knew the man needed help and he gave it to him. He saved the Judean man's life and paid for his care. He saw a man in need of help and he gave it to him. Jesus said that's what it means to love one's neighbor as yourself."

I preached the same sermon to the second service and also to the Vietnamese service. At the conclusion of the Vietnamese service I added a comment. "Brothers and sisters, we have neighbors who need our help. The children many of you met a few days ago were taken from their homes in Vietnam with the intention of being sold into slavery. They were abused and beaten by evil men who didn't care if they lived or died, they were only interested in the money they would make when they sold them. I ask you to pray for them. Search your hearts and see if you can help them in any way. Be their Samaritan."

CHAPTER 22

The Adoptions—Pham Bin Minh, Attorney at Law

An hour after the Vietnamese service concluded, we were ready to start the adoption process. Pastor Boa and his wife set the example by adopting two sisters, Jade and her younger sister, Moon. It took less than thirty minutes to complete the process.

I had a team of people who assisted me in the adoption process and ten tables were set up with nine other attorneys who were associates of mine. We also had notaries available to help document the adoptions. The pastor's wife and several other Vietnamese women from the church, helped matching up the children with the people who wished to adopt them. They also passed out refreshments to everyone. It was a busy afternoon and evening.

We finished up by 9:00pm. About seventy of the children had been adopted by their new parents, more than I had anticipated. They left as soon as the adoption process was completed. That left thirty-four older children who weren't selected. You could see the disappointment in their faces, a few were crying and returned to their quarters when it became obvious they weren't going to be chosen.

All of the lawyers and notaries had left, with the exception of myself and my notary. Pastor Bao and his wife brought the thirty-four out and the pastor told them, "Please don't be sad. We have a surprise for you. Cam and I are going to adopt all of you right now. We will become your new parents. You will live here in the church with us until we can arrange for more permanent housing. Many of you will become adults in a few years and we will do our best to prepare you for living in America. We will begin by teaching you to speak, read and write English. Now, please line up, from the youngest to the oldest so we can get you adopted."

Once the adoption process was completed, their sadness changed to cautious joy. They had been disappointed so many times, they weren't really sure if we would follow through with our promise.

It had been a long night. I sent my notary home but I wanted to speak with Pastor Bao and his wife before I left. It seemed like tonight was an evening full of surprises for so many people but there was one surprise left.

When they were done getting the children settled in, they joined me at one of the tables. The pastor said to me, "I want to thank you for the miracle you performed tonight. Without you, this night would never have happened. Without you, we would never have been able to keep our promise…"

Before he could continue, we heard an outside door open, then close, followed by the click of boots on the tile floor. We all looked up to see Joshua walking toward us. Now, I was surprised, not by his presence but by the expression on his face. He was smiling! Granted, it wasn't a huge smile but was definitely more than a grin. I couldn't remember seeing him smile more than two or three times in all the years I have known him.

We all stood up to greet him and Cam gave him a hug. "It's so good to see you," she said. "I'm sorry you didn't get here sooner. The children would have loved to see their savior one last time."

We all sat back down as Joshua said, "Actually, it's better this way. If they had seen me, they might associate my appearance with all the trauma they had lived through. So, tell me, how did it go?"

"It went exceptionally well," answered the pastor. "We found homes for over seventy of the children. Unfortunately, thirty-four weren't adopted, at least not by our Vietnamese families. Cam and I decided to adopt all thirty-four ourselves. They were all in their teens, close to becoming adults. We plan to offer them some basic schooling to prepare them for that day. We made a promise to you that all of them would be adopted. With your help, the help of Pham Bin Minh and our Vietnamese families, we were able to keep that promise."

Joshua stared at the pastor for a few moments, his expression unreadable. "I'm overjoyed you kept your promise. I don't get to say overjoyed often. I'm sure your church families will cherish their adopted children."

He looked from the pastor to his wife and then at me. I could tell he had shifted to his serious mode. "How are you going to provide for your thirty-four new children?"

"Actually, it's thirty-six. We adopted Jade and Moon too," interrupted Cam.

"God will provide," said the pastor. "We really don't know how we will move forward from today but I'm confident God will provide us with what we need."

"How long can you keep your new family in the church basement?" Joshua asked. "Have you spoken to your senior pastor yet?"

"No, he returns two days from now. I will speak to him then," the pastor replied.

Joshua stared at the pastor and shook his head. "That's not going to work for me. I have to leave early tomorrow morning and I need to know everything is taken care of before I go."

The pastor and his wife seemed to pale at Joshua's comments. They looked like they were searching for something to say that would appease him. Before they could speak, Joshua, turned to me and said, "Tell them, Pham."

"Tell us what?" asked Cam with a tension filled voice.

I cleared my throat and began, "We knew some of the children wouldn't be adopted. We weren't sure how many that would be. We also knew they would be the older children. So, Joshua gave me orders to set this up."

The pastor looked confused, "Set what up? What did you do?"

"An anonymous organization has donated a substantial amount of money for you to establish a boarding school for immigrant Vietnamese children. The school will initially have rooms for up to fifty boarders. There will be classrooms to accommodate up to two hundred children including day students as well as the boarders. This school will teach the basics: how to speak, write and read English, basic math, those kinds of things. There will be no tuition fees and study material will be provided. Oh and before I forget, the building already exists and your thirty-four children can move in tomorrow. Teachers and staff are already on site. Here's the deed, I'll have all the other paperwork for you tomorrow."

Cam and Pastor Boa sat in stunned silence. Tears were streaming down Cam's cheeks and the pastor had to swallow three times before he could talk, "How…when…" he gave up and just shook his head.

In a soft voice, Joshua said, "You were right. God will provide. He instructed me to make this happen. I was happy to oblige. I have to leave you now but I will check in with you from time to time to see how things are going. If you need anything, anything at all please contact Pham. He will always know where I am."

Joshua stood, Cam ran to him and hugged him tightly. "Thank you so much. You will be in our prayers daily. Be careful and God bless you."

As he walked out the door, all the pastor could say was "There goes the good, no, the BEST Samaritan."

CHAPTER 23

Moving On-Special Agent Joshua Brown

I received my orders earlier that night. I was to be at the Portland Air National Guard Base at 2330 hours to board a C-17 and fly to Memphis, Tennessee. I would be taking my ride with me. I really liked having my car with me on my missions. It was a highly modified Humvee. I did all of the modifications, well most of them. Some of the mods were so sophisticated it took a team of specialists to make it happen. Think of it as a Prius on steroids, lots of steroids.

I arrived at Portland Air National Guard Base shortly after 2130 hours. The Guard Base is co-located with Portland International Airport and situated on the south side of the runways. I had almost two hours to wait and planned to use the time to write up my AAR, more commonly known as the After Action Report. I found a quiet corner in the small cafeteria, grabbed a sandwich and drink and sat at a table near the windows overlooking the active runway. I still get a thrill watching the birds land and takeoff, especially the F-15s based at Portland.

I opened up my laptop and began to dictate the report. I really love the feature that lets me talk to my computer and it does all the typing. Whenever I try to type anything, I'm attacked by a bad case of fat-finger syndrome. Besides, I can talk three times faster than a good typist could pound it out. I keep telling myself it's more efficient.

After Action Report Summary

The Portland Human Trafficking mission was successfully concluded at 0930 hours this date. Over a hundred Vietnamese children between the ages of eight to fifteen were saved from potential slavery. All were adopted into Vietnamese families and are in the process of acclimatizing to the American culture. All of the people associated with the transport of the children by container ship from Singapore to Portland have been either imprisoned or killed. The members of the Bing Hop Tong involved in the transference of the children from the shipping containers to the slave owners have been neutralized. I was forced to eliminate nine of their soldiers who attempted to keep me from rescuing the children from the shipping containers. The next day, the leaders of the Bing Hop and several of their members were executed by four well-armed men. The remainder of the Tong left Portland and I believe it is safe to say they no longer exist as an organization in the Portland area.

The four men who committed the execution of the Bing Hop were in turn killed by Portland SWAT before they could leave the Portland area. From the police report of the incident, they received an anonymous tip of the four men's location. When confronted by police, they chose to fight rather than surrender. A gun fight took place and all four were shot and died at the scene.

I recommend commendations be made to the following people: Detectives Joey Hong and Bill Cody form the Portland Police, Pastor Bao and his wife Cam from the Grace Bible Church in northwest Portland, Pham Bin Minh, attorney at law and Mark Riley, security guard at Portland's Terminal 6. Without the assistance of these people, a successful completion of this mission wouldn't have been possible. They all went above and beyond to assist me.

I finished the more detailed report, encrypted it along with the summary and emailed it to my leader. I got another bottle of water and sat facing the windows as a flight of F-15s began their takeoff roll down the runway. They left two at a time, side by side.

Half way down they went to afterburners and bright yellow-white fire shot out of their jet exhausts. I could hear the roar of the burners and see the shock diamonds in the flames as they lifted off and pulled up into a near vertical climb. In less than a minute they were out of sight. Then the second two did a repeat performance. Outstanding!

I had been so focused on the fighters, I hadn't noticed my C-17 landing on an adjacent runway. It was on the taxi way heading for the ramp. I stood up, finished my drink and threw the empty bottle into the recycle can. I secured my laptop in my duffle and headed for my vehicle. I flashed my creds as I drove through the security gate and headed for the C-17. It had stopped on the ramp, shut off its engines and was lowering its rear ramp. One of the crew motioned for me to drive up into the belly of the beast and I complied. Fifteen minutes later they had secured my vehicle for the flight while the aircraft was being fueled. I didn't actually see them refueling but the distinct odor of JP-4 is very obvious.

I had walked up the ramp to watch the crew take care of my vehicle and was met by one of the flight crew. "Are you Special Agent Brown?" the major asked.

"Yes sir, I am. Here are my credentials and my orders."

The major stood under one of the interior lights and checked everything thoroughly. When he was satisfied I was who I said I was, he directed me to a small compartment, upfront near the cockpit. It had three rows of first-class seats, complete with fold down-trays. The major said, "The seats fold all the way down in case you want to catch a nap. We also have Wi-Fi in case you want to work on your computer or watch a video. There's a cabinet with snacks, water and soda and there's a head behind the door at the rear of the compartment. You're our only passenger tonight so you have the compartment all to yourself. We should have you on the ground at Memphis in about four hours depending on the weather. Any questions?"

"Nope. Thanks for the tour, Major." I stored my duffle and took a window seat in the back row, except this was a cargo plane and they didn't have any windows. I heard the ramp coming up, followed by the sound of the first of the four turbofans beginning to spool up.

After the four engines were at idle, a voice came over the PA. "We're cleared to taxi. Secure and strap in. We're number three for takeoff."

Ten minutes later, we were accelerating down the runway. Being in a cargo jet isn't like flying in a passenger plane. They save weight by neglecting to put in any sound reducing material. As the engines ramped up to full power they produced a deafening roar. Once we were airborne and climbing, the pilot cut back on the power slightly so it was now possible to not only hear the noise of the retracting landing gear, you could feel the vibrations as the gear locked into place and the doors shut. This was followed by a loud whining sound as the flaps were retracted into the wings. In ten minutes, maybe fifteen, we were steadily climbing to our cruise altitude. The noise level was then down to a dull roar. Did all that noise and bouncing around bother me? Absolutely not. I had turned out the cabin light and was sound asleep sometime between taxing to the active runway and our takeoff. I learned in the Marines to ignore the things that can't kill you and sleep whenever you can and I did.

I awoke when the C-17 touched down at the Memphis airport. With the time zone changes, we landed just after sunrise. There's nothing like the roar of the thrust reversers abruptly slowing the plane to wake you from a sound sleep. It was a good thing I had strapped in before going to sleep.

When we had slowed sufficiently to exit the runway and begin to taxi to the ramp, I unstrapped and used the head, washed up and brushed my teeth. By the time the plane stopped and the rear cargo door began to lower, I had my duffle in hand and left the compartment.

I watched as the crew began unstrapping my vehicle. The major, apparently the official greeter of the plane, walked up to me to say good-bye. Ten minutes later I was in my ride heading out of the terminal.

As I passed an IHOP, I decided to stop for breakfast and to review my new mission plan. I took a booth in the back corner of the restaurant, placed my order and opened up my laptop and began to read. I wanted to get a feel for what the mission would entail. I would do a detailed study of the plan after I had gotten settled in Jericho, about a two- hour drive from Memphis.

When the food arrived, I closed the laptop and started eating. I like IHOP, they serve great food at reasonable prices and they're everywhere. As I ate, I thought about the parameters of the mission. This was going to be challenging, probably the most challenging of any of my previous missions. I was going to need help, I had a few people in mind.

I finished eating but decided to have another cup of coffee and get some background information on the real Jericho, Mississippi. I'm a big fan of Ace Atkins who has written a series of crime novels set in Jericho. His books focus on some pretty unsavory characters with a lot of crime, sex and nasty language thrown in for good measure. The main character is, Sheriff Quinn Colson, a former Army Ranger. He's the good guy surrounded by some really mean and evil men and women. Sheriff Colson kind of reminds me of myself, except he's a white man who was an Army Ranger and is now a sheriff, while I'm a black man, a Marine and a Federal Agent. I guess the similarities aren't so similar after all.

My Google search of Jericho, Mississippi, reveals the town is unincorporated and governed by the Union County Board of Supervisors. There hasn't been a census taken in recent memory but the town's population is estimated to me around 10,000. The breakdown of the population is thought to be sixty percent white, thirty percent black, and ten percent Hispanic and Indian. The town is located in northeast Mississippi and lies north of a Choctaw reservation. The geography of the land is described as rolling hills.

I finished my coffee, paid my bill, got in my vehicle and entered Jericho into the GPS. Nineteen different states had a town named Jericho and it asked me to choose one. I selected Mississippi. The map popped up on my color display and I checked the route. Take I-22 out of Memphis to US Highway 45 then turn left at Guntown (interesting name) to state route 370 which takes me through the middle of Jericho…in Mississippi. I liked the route. It would give me a chance to check out the landscape that surrounded the town on at least three sides.

I pushed the Go button on the display, strapped into my seat, fired up my ride, checked the instruments to make sure they were all in the green then turned on my favorite song, *Born to be Wild,* and headed out to the highway.

PART 3

CHAPTER 24

Recon—Joshua Brown

I was cruising southeast on the I-22 in diesel mode. I had the cruise control set at 75mph and the tunes blasting away with the A/C set at 70F. Outside it was hot and humid, not that I minded too much. I'd spent plenty of time in much worse climate but If I could avoid it, why not? I had my combat gear lying on the passenger seat with my new weapons, two Desert Eagle 50 AE semiautomatics. After I saw a video of a professional shooter firing five rounds of 300 grain bullets at 1,475 feet per second in eight tenths of a second, I was sold. I managed to sneak in some target practice at a range in Portland. I did some serious damage to the targets. I had to pay for replacement targets, but it was well worth the cost to get comfortable with the guns. I kept one in a holster attached to my driver side door and the other in a similar rig on the center console.

It was a little under an hour and a half when I came to the turnoff to highway 45. It was another ten minutes to Guntown (I love that name. I'm going to have to check that place out). A few minutes later, I made the left turn onto state route 370 and pulled into the parking lot for the Choctaw Burial Site.

This is going to require some historical background. When Europeans began settling America in the 16th century, the Choctaw were living in the southeastern United States, largely in the area that was to become Mississippi. In the war between the British and the French during the 18th century, the Choctaw allied with the French. The French were defeated in the French and Indian War (1754-63) and some of the Choctaw land was taken from them by the British, forcing many to move westward in search of new lands.

During the 18th century the Choctaw were very prosperous and their land holdings spread across central Mississippi. However, when the United States of America came into being, their desire for expansion resulted in the Choctaw being forced to sign treaties that ceded much of their land to the United States. Through a series of treaties between 1801 and 1830, the Choctaw Nation ceded over 23 million acres of land.

Many of the Choctaw were moved to reservations in Oklahoma, however some still remained in the central part of Mississippi, with one important exception.

In northeastern Mississippi, less than ten miles from the town of Jericho, ten acres of land remained in Choctaw possession. It was a burial site they refused to give up. It was considered holy ground, sacred to them.

The parking lot was right off SR 370 but the actual burial site was about two miles north, located on a high hill over a hundred feet above the surrounding area.

An eight-foot block fence had surrounded the grounds to keep out anyone who might attempt to vandalize the burial site. Four Choctaw police from the southern reservations were on duty 24/7 to further ensure the site was secured.

Within the last decade, the Choctaw had established a museum adjacent to the parking lot available to the public. An annual ceremony was held to honor the spirits of the departed Choctaw. The public was allowed to attend but no one except the Choctaw were allowed inside the actual burial site.

Three years ago, a team of archaeologists unearthed some material that indicated the site near Jericho was in fact not an actual burial site. That finding was later substantiated by other archaeologists who discovered evidence found at another nearby site. It turns out the supposed burial site was an area of mass graves for the bodies of soldiers from the French and Indian War. It contained the remains of British and French as well as Choctaw men who had been killed during that bloody conflict.

The question that everyone wanted answered was: What happens to the ten acres of land? Who owns it? That question was quickly answered: The Choctaw Nation still owned the land. What did they want to do with the ten acres? The answer was obvious: build a huge resort hotel and casino.

There were already several casinos built on Choctaw reservations but the burial site would allow for the first casino in northern Mississippi, almost a hundred miles away from the others.

I got out of my vehicle and stood in the parking lot, looking at what the Choctaw, along with their sponsors, had built. There was only one road leading up to the new twelve-foot wall which surrounded the many buildings that made up the resort hotel and casino. I noticed a large number of jet-black buses and limos with the casino logo painted on in blazing red letters. They were parked on one corner of the enormous parking lot. Apparently, the only way in or out was by resort vehicles. I could barely see the top of the actual buildings. I thought to myself, *In any battle, you always want the high ground.*

I took out my phone and began taking pictures of the parking lot and the two-lane entrance/exit road with the security barricade placed at the road entrance near the parking lot.

After I'd shot about fifty stills, I opened the back door of my ride and took out my Skyline drone. To my way of thinking, this was about the coolest tech I'd seen in a very long time. Folded up, it fit in the palm of my hand. Unfolded, it was about two feet wide. It had four props that could lift the drone to over 200 feet above the ground. It had a high-resolution video camera and all you needed to control it was your smart phone. Best of all, it cost less than $100. I had a dozen of them in a box in the back of my vehicle.

I was in the process of unfolding the drone and getting it ready for launch when I noticed a very large white guy coming my way from a single-wide trailer on the other side of the lot. He had to weigh three-fifty if he weighed an ounce. He wore a very dirty white

T-shirt with the words Dolly's Hide Out written across the chest and a pair of torn-up jeans. I wasn't sure how he held up his jeans, his monstrous belly hung over the waistband and hid any belt he might have been wearing.

He took off his ball cap and wiped the sweat off his forehead with his forearm, squinted at me and said in a very pronounced southern drawl, "What cha all doin' here, boy? Dis here's private property. You need to get your black ass outta here pronto."

I looked him in the eye and said, "My black ass is staying right where it is. Who are you and what makes you think I will pay any attention to you...boy?"

He squinted at me, then snarled, "You better watch your lip. Open your mouth again like dat and I be tearing it off your ugly face."

I laughed at him and showed him my credentials, my new credentials. Then said, "Can you read, you big tub of guts? I suppose not, so let me tell you what they say, I'm Joshua Brown, special agent for the Bureau of Indian Affairs. You're keeping me from finishing my inspection of the resort site. If you're not out of my sight in ten seconds, I will have the sheriff haul your substantial lily white ass into jail. You understand me…boy?"

He took a threatening step toward me beginning to mumble, "No damn nig…"

Before he could finish that word, I whipped out my Desert Eagle 50 AE and pointed it at his right eye ball. "Say it and it will be the last word you ever speak."

His knees buckled slightly and for a moment, he looked shocked. But he quickly recovered and said, "You bluffing, I can call you anything I damn well please and you won't shoot me. I know my rights…"

I fired two quick shots between his legs, a hair's width from his private parts. He fell to his knees and fainted.

I left him lying there while I launched the drone, maneuvering it up the hill and over the resort site as three men came running out of the trailer toward us.

I ignored them and set up the drone to do a slow grid-search pattern over the entire resort, taking videos for me to check out later. I turned my attention to the three men who were just reaching Tub of Guts, who still remained motionless on the ground.

One I thought might be Choctaw, the other two were white men. They all appeared annoyed. "Did you kill him?" asked the Choctaw.

"Nope," I answered, "Just a couple of warning shots. He's not even wounded."

"What's that smell?...Oh my god, he pooped his pants!" said one of the white men who had kneeled down to check the fat man out. He scrambled to his feet and backed away quickly while he covered his nose and mouth with his hand.

They all stepped back from Tub of Guts and ignored him as best they could. All three men were carrying weapons and one began to reach for his.

"I wouldn't do that. Just stand easy while I show you my creds, okay?"

They nodded reluctantly and I pulled out my cred pack again and handed it to the man who I thought still might draw his weapon. He took it with his right hand, which prevented him from grabbing his gun. I really don't like killing people, especially for no good reason.

The three men huddled together looking at my credentials as I said, "You all should have received an email letting you know I was coming and to let me tour the site."

The Choctaw shook his head. "We aren't the normal security men. They were sent away on some special business. I think it was in Portland, not sure which state. We were brought in to sub as security until they return. No one told us you were coming."

I nodded. "I'm pretty sure the regular security team isn't coming back."

Tub of Guts began moaning, then opened his eyes and saw everyone watching him. "Can you help me up, Clyde," he asked reaching out his hand towards the closest man.

"I don't think so, Beaner. You messed yourself. I think you're on your own."

He looked at the other two men who quickly looked away. He struggled to his feet and stared at me and shouted, "This ain't over. I get you back, you hear me. I get you back!"

The Choctaw shouted at him, "Shut up, Beaner. Go clean yourself up."

The monstrously fat man turned away and staggered toward the trailer with his legs spread wide.

I told the remaining three, "I'll be leaving soon, as soon as my drone has finished its sweep of the resort. I'll be back tomorrow morning at ten to do my walk around. It will probably take all day. Anyone have any problem with that?"

They all shook their heads, turned and began walking back to the trailer. A thought occurred to me. "Keep Beaner away from me tomorrow. If he gets in my face again, I'll have to hurt him."

Thirty minutes later my drone automatically returned to where I'd launched it. I picked it up, folded the four arms and returned it to its case. I would look at the playback on my iPad when I was settled in my hotel room.

I powered up my vehicle and drove out of the parking lot, heading toward the town of Jericho. Ten minutes later, I saw a sign that read **Welcome To Jericho, Hope You Enjoy Your Stay.** Underneath, someone had scrawled Who Cares?

I switched to electric mode and the diesel immediately shut down. I didn't want the noise of the diesel to attract attention to my arrival. Hotel reservations for me had been made in advance. I pulled into the parking lot, picked up my duffle, locked my ride and headed into the hotel.

I squared away my gear and called room service for lunch: double cheese burger with all the fixings, French fries and a large Coke Zero (have to cut down on the calories somewhere).

While I waited for the food, I set up my iPad and installed the memory disc from the drone. I connected the iPad to the large flat screen TV so I could get a better look at the new resort. The video was crystal clear and using the iPad controls, I was able to replay or pause various images I found interesting. I was half way through when I heard a knock at my door and a muffled voice, "Room service."

I picked up one of my Desert Eagles and walked to the door and opened it a crack. There was a young man with a white bag in one hand and a large plastic cup in the other. I could see the name of the bag: Fillin' Station Diner.

I put the gun on the dresser next to the door and opened it wide. The youth walked in and placed the bag and drink on my table next to my iPad. He turned, smiled and said, "That will be seven dollars, sir."

I gave him a ten and told him to keep the change. He thanked me and headed for the door but stopped when I asked, "The hotel doesn't have a restaurant?"

"No sir. But it's no problem for us to go to the diner, it's just across the street."

I gestured to the bag and asked, "Is it really called The Fillin' Station Diner?"

He giggled. "You must be a fan of Ace Atkins' books. Yes sir, that's its real name."

He left and I sat down to eat. It was one of the best cheese burgers I had ever eaten in recent memory. I was really enjoying my lunch when there was another knock on the door. *I wonder what the kid forgot,* I thought to myself. I wiped my mouth and walked to the door, picking up the Desert Eagle on my way.

I opened the door, my weapon held out of sight, and saw a tall, muscular man in a brown uniform shirt with a silver star on the chest. He said, "Are you Mr. Joshua Brown?"

"I am," I said. Then asked, "Are you Sheriff Quinn Colson?"

He shook his head, then said with a straight face, "Sorry. I'm not him but I must look like him because people are always asking me that. May I come in?

I laid the weapon back on the dresser, opened the door and he walked in. "Have a seat, Sheriff. What can I do for you?"

"I'll stand. This won't take too long." He quickly scanned the room, his gaze pausing on the Desert Eagle, then continuing his scan. "Are you the owner of the heavily modified Humvee parked in the hotel parking lot?"

"Yes sir, I am. Is there a problem?"

"Not with your vehicle but someone was trying to mess with it. A witness said the man attempted to use a slim jim to gain access to your car, presumably to steal it or steal something inside it. The witness said he heard 'a very loud electric snap' and the man fell back onto the ground, unconscious. He's currently being treated by EMTs. Could you explain what happened to him?"

I tried to keep from smiling. "Sure Sheriff. That was an example of my antitheft device. Anyone who attempts to enter my vehicle while the device is active receives an electric shock similar to what one would experience when hit with a two-hundred volt stun gun. It's not lethal unless they are wearing a pacemaker. He should be fine in a few hours."

"Is that device commercially available?" he asked with a serious expression.

"Not yet," I answered, then added, "perhaps to prevent any further occurrences, I could park my vehicle in a secured area and rent a car while I'm visiting Jericho."

He smiled broadly and replied, "That's an excellent idea. In fact, you can store your vehicle in our secure impound yard. Only one of my deputies and myself have access. It wouldn't cost you anything and it would minimize the number of EMT calls."

He gave me instructions to the impound yard and left me to finish my lunch. I took my ride to the yard, checked it out to make sure it met my requirements for secure storage, locked it up and activated the antitheft device. *Why take any risks you don't have to?*

The sheriff, Sheriff Davy Jones, took me to the car rental company and I selected one I liked. I drove back to the hotel and continued my review of the drone video.

The next morning, I headed out to the resort. First, I stopped at the Fillin' Station Diner to buy a breakfast sandwich and a cup of coffee which I ate on the way out of town. I missed my vehicle. I felt kind of naked driving a pickup truck but it was less conspicuous.

I thought about what I watched last evening and was anxious to confirm close up what I'd seen in the drone video. My first reaction was that somebody, or more likely a group of somebodies, had spent a boat load of money on this venture. It exceeded anything I'd ever seen in Vegas. I couldn't understand how they could possibly recoup their investment in this sleepy little burg in northeast Mississippi.

I pulled into the resort parking lot and was met by a group of people. Fortunately, Tub of Guts Beaner wasn't one of them. In addition to the three other security guards, there were another three dressed in suits and ties. Sheriff Jones was there too and he didn't look very happy.

I got out of the truck and nodded at the group. "Good morning, gentlemen. How may I help you?" I asked in a friendly voice.

One of the suits, the oldest and I assumed the leader of the group, said to the sheriff, "Arrest this man for attempted murder of one of our employees."

Apparently, the sheriff hadn't been told this was going to happened. He turned to the old man in charge and said, "Wait a minute, supervisor. Before I arrest anyone, I need to have some reasonable evidence that indicates Mr. Brown attempted to kill Beaner."

The supervisor sighed and said to the sheriff as if he were speaking to a child, "Of course we have evidence. We have three witnesses that will swear they saw this man," he pointed at me with a long boney finger, "fire his gun at Beaner when Beaner asked him to leave."

"Not true and I can prove it," I replied before anyone could say anything else. "I fired my weapon in self-defense after the man you call Beaner threatened me with bodily harm. And there were no witnesses to any of this until after I had fired my weapon. By the way, if I had wanted to murder Beaner he would be dead."

The supervisor became enraged and shouted at me, "Liar! You're a damned liar."

"I have video from my body cam that proves what I just said. My question to you, supervisor, is why are you trying to keep me from examining the resort? What are you trying to hide?"

Apparently, the supervisor wasn't used to having somebody argue with him. His face flushed a bright crimson as he turned to the sheriff and shouted, "Do your duty, Sheriff. I want this man in jail immediately!"

The sheriff shook his head and said, "Sorry. Until I check out Mr. Brown's body cam video, I'm not going to arrest him."

"Would you all like to see it now? It's in my iPad in the truck," I said, as I watched the supervisor's expression change. He became angrier and began shouting, "Liar! I don't care what fake evidence he claims to have, I want him off this site immediately or you're out of a job, Sheriff."

The sheriff remained calm as he replied, "First, the position of sheriff of Union County is an elected position. You can't fire me.

Secondly, if you're so sure he's lying, why not watch the video to see for yourself and thirdly, if his video confirms what he said, I'm going to have to arrest your three security men for lying to an officer of the law."

The supervisor stared at the sheriff for a long moment and growled, "This isn't over, Sheriff. This isn't over by a long shot."

He turned abruptly and headed for his limo, the other two supervisors close behind him. The sheriff and I and the three security men watched the limo roar out of the parking lot, burning rubber as they left.

The three security men were silent and sullen as I cued up the replay of the dance between me and Tub of Guts. When it was finished, the Choctaw was the first to speak.

"The supervisor is the liar. We never said we saw you try to shoot Beaner. We told him what we saw after the gun shots. He told us we were wrong and if we didn't agree to the story he made up, he would fire us. We needed the work so we just shut up and let him do the talking. If you hadn't mentioned this body cam video, he would have had us sign sworn statements you tried to kill Beaner."

"Sheriff," I said, "I'm not up on Mississippi law but I'm pretty sure since these three men didn't sign any kind of complaint or even verbally say I tried to kill Beaner, I don't think you can arrest them. Is that right?"

He nodded but didn't say anything, waiting for what he knew was coming.

"And," I continued, "It seems to me the supervisor is the one who is guilty of making false claims of attempted murder and trying to get these three men to lie for him under duress."

The sheriff nodded and waited for my final question.

"Can you arrest him on those charges?" I asked.

He shrugged his shoulders and answered, "Yes I can but it wouldn't be in my best interest to do so. This is Mississippi, things are done differently here than the rest of America. It's who you know that counts and the supervisor has lots of friends in high places including judges. No judge would ever find him guilty or send him to jail."

We all stood quietly, considering the best way to move forward. After a moment I suggested, "How about we give the story to the press. Is there a newspaper or TV station that would run this story?"

"Yes, there are," he replied, "but it would generate a lot of law suits and probably a number of missing persons who are never seen again. Like I said, this is Mississippi. Things are done differently here. You won a battle here this morning. You didn't get arrested and you still get to check out the resort. Is that going to be enough for you?"

I shrugged. "For now, at least. What about you men?" I asked the three security men.

"We'll get fired but the job was only temporary anyway. At least we're not going to jail, right sheriff?" asked Choctaw.

"Right. No jail time. Tell Beaner he's off the hook too."

"What next?" I asked. "Can we still check out the resort today?"

I noticed a slight smile appeared on Choctaw's face. "We've never been inside. Chances are we never will. This place is for high rollers, millionaires. We heard rumors this place will be the sin city of the southeastern United States. Supposed to put Vegas to shame. Everything goes. I got the keys. I want to see if it's true?"

We all got into one of the limos and headed up the road to the new and improved Sin City.

CHAPTER 25

Sodom and Gomorrah—Joshua Brown

The five of us started up the road in one of the resort limos. Sheriff Jones and myself were in the front and the three security temps, Choctaw, Clyde and Jerry sat in the spacious back seats.

The entrance had two ten-foot high gates made of wood and black iron. "How do we get in?" I asked.

The Choctaw, who had asked me to call him Bear, replied, "Push the left garage door button on the rearview mirror."

Sheriff Jones was driving. He reached up and touched the button. We watched as the doors began to swing inward. Bear said, "Lucky break. I wasn't sure it would work."

The gates were located near the southwest corner of the wall. As we drove inside, the first thing we noticed was the immense fountain in the middle of the plaza. It was supposed to have waterfalls and jets but the fountain was dry. The road made a circle around the fountain then headed down to the parking lot. The drone video had shown the fountain and the turnaround where the guests were supposed to exit their vehicles. I assumed the buses or limos returned to the parking lot to pick up more guests or to take those who were leaving to the parking lot. Sheriff Jones parked our limo next to the entrance to the resort area and we walked into the lobby area of the hotel.

The lobby was enormous and very plush. My entire hotel in Jericho would have fit nicely into one of its corners. We spent some time checking it out. There were more fountains (also dry) and massive marble columns, clusters of very comfortable chairs, love seats and sofas covered in soft leather with wood and brass details. There were also several larger than life nude statues intermingled with the furniture and huge paintings with intricate gold leaf frames hung on the walls.

Looking up, the ceiling must have been three stories high with seven (I counted them) crystal chandeliers hanging from gold fixtures. An open mezzanine was along the rear wall which included what looked like a spacious lounge that probably served adult beverages.

What was missing was a registration counter where the guests could check in. Instead, two story high French doors with decorative trim opened into another enormous room. A large sign lit with blinking red lights read: **Orientation Room, Please Enter Now.**

So, we all entered…now.

There must have been at least two hundred chairs facing a raised platform at the other end of the room. It was dark and I used the flashlight on my smart phone to search for wall switches. The sheriff found a panel next to the French doors and opened it. He started pushing buttons and eventually, soft indirect lighting filled the room. We noticed someone standing on the platform with his back to the rows of chairs. He turned around and acted surprised to see us. "Oh, hello there. Why don't you all take a seat and I'll begin your orientation. This will take about twenty minutes so get some refreshments from the table before you sit down,"

He was a good looking man dressed in a dark suit with a red tie. I'd say he was in his late thirties or early forties. There was just a touch of gray around his temples and he had a warm, friendly smile as he gestured at a blank wall where the refreshments should have been.

"He isn't real, is he?" said Bear.

"Must be a hologram," said Clyde.

Mr. Holo waited for a few minutes and then said, "Okay, let's get started."

We quickly sat down in the first row as he began his pitch. The room lights dimmed and most of the stage went dark except where he was standing. "Let me be the first to welcome you to this new resort. It's been called by many names, like Sin City East, Babylon or, one of my favorites, Sodom and Gomorrah. So far, we haven't given it a name. Since the ground the resort stands on is owned by the Choctaw Nation, we're waiting for them to name it.

"All the names I mentioned should give you the idea this is an adults only resort and you'd be right. No one under the age of eighteen is allowed to enter. But I'm here to tell you this isn't like any adult resort you've ever seen, heard of or even dreamed about. We have everything you could possibly want. Let me tell you about just a few of them."

He paused for effect then said, "If you are a gambler, welcome to Gambler's Paradise. Our casino has every form of gaming opportunity known to man and few new ones thrown in. Just take a look!"

The man's image blinked out and the stage became a panorama of slot machines, poker tables, roulette wheels, craps tables and on and on and on. As we watched the three-dimensional image slowly drift by, you could hear all the casino sounds in stereo, especially the ding-ding-ding of jackpots being won.

As the casino faded the host returned and said, "Maybe you're a party animal and like to dance to the latest music while you have some drinks with your friends to the wee small hours of the morning. Look no further, my friends, we have something for everyone in our five, count 'em, five night clubs. If you're into country music, we've got it." He paused as the stage was filled with a band playing *Friends in Low Places* and people dancing the Texas two-step all dressed in cowboy getup, cowgirl too, of course.

As that scene faded, the host appeared. "If you like rock and roll, we've got it in spades. How about soul music? We've got that too. Or maybe you're into watching beautiful, almost naked, women swinging around on brass poles or giving you erotic lap dances, this is the place to be."

Each time he mentioned a different type of music, the stage was filled with the scene of a different club with people dancing and drinking and having a great time. When they got to pole dancing they seemed to linger longer with very close-up views of the dancers. When that faded out, the host changed the tone of his voice. It was deeper, almost seductive.

"Or maybe you are just interested in sex. We can accommodate whatever you prefer. From romantic one-on-one evenings to down and dirty group orgies and everything in between. If you prefer same sex activities, that's fine with us. If you want to bring your own partner, be our guest. Or if you prefer, we can match you up with one of our hosts or hostesses." As he spoke, images began to appear of beautiful women and handsome men. All were totally naked. Every race was presented, Blacks, Hispanics, Asian, Indians and Whites. All were well proportioned as they moved from one suggestive pose to another. I heard Clyde whisper to no one in particular, "Look at the tatas on that one! Lord save me."

Our host added, "Perhaps you are a little on the kinky side and enjoy certain types of fetishes. Well who doesn't from time to time?"

As he spoke, a young Asian girl appeared on the stage, dressed in a school girl uniform, she was very slender and looked to be a very young teenager. An older white man approached her and in spite of her resistance, began to undress her.

"Stop!" I shouted. I was on my feet before I realized I had pulled my weapon and was aiming it at the image of the old man. I holstered the gun and slumped back onto my chair. I was shaking with rage.

When I'd yelled Stop the presentation had shut down and the house lights came on. Everyone was staring at me, shocked by my behavior. Sheriff Jones asked, "You okay Joshua?"

I took a deep breath, then exhaled, forcing myself to relax. "Sorry everyone. The girl looked like someone I know. Seeing her in that situation triggered a reflex reaction. It won't happen again. Can we fast forward? I've seen enough sex for tonight."

Clyde looked a little disappointed but nodded his head in agreement as did the others.

When the program started up again, Mr. Holo had changed gears. He was alone on the stage and the house lights were brighter now as he said, "Let's talk about how much all this is going to cost you." He paused for a beat as he looked around the room of empty chairs, smiled, then said, "Well, I've got some good news and some bad news. First, the good news, your money is no good here, except when you want to tip somebody for excellent service. The bad news is, you better have a credit card with a high limit. We're not talking about millions of dollars, at least not for our average guest. Our starting point is a thousand.

"Let me give you some examples how this works. When you leave here you will be going to the Check In counter, where a real human being will ask you for your driver's license, that's just to make sure you're over eighteen and your credit card. We take Visa, Master Card, American Express and Discover. Then let's say you plan on staying no more than four hours. We would then bill your card for a thousand dollars but we don't submit it until you leave. In return we give you a resort debit card. Let me emphasize this next comment. DO NOT LOSE YOUR DEBIT CARD. If you do, please notify one our hosts or hostesses immediately and we will block any further charges.

"Let's say you want to gamble for a while, you like to play the slots, so you slip your resort debit card into the machine, decide how much you want to bet and have at it. When you win a jackpot, it's credited to your card. When you don't win, it's debited to your card. It works the same everywhere you go in the resort. If you want to have a few drinks and watch the ladies as they pole dance, give the bartender your card. Every time you order another drink, your card is debited. By the way, there's no charge to watch pole dancing but if you decide you want a lap dance in our VIP suite, just insert your card in the slot on the arm of the chair. You can tip the dancer with cash or add it as a debit to your card."

He turned and started to walk slowly across the platform to an exit with a blinking light above it. He said as he walked, "Instead of taking your valuable time and bore you with any further details, there're flyers at the Check-In counter that give you all the details. One last comment. Everything is permitted here except brawling and murder, so enjoy yourselves to the fullest."

Mr. Holo vanished and the room lights got brighter. We walked through the doors into an empty room with the words **Check In Here** blinking above numerous counter spaces. As promised, there were flyers on the counter near each location. We all took one and began our tour of the rest of the resort.

We exited Check In into an enormous space. To our left was hotel registration for those who planned to stay overnight or a few days, perhaps a week or more if you have a credit card with an exceptionally high credit limit. The flyer mentioned, condos were available for those who wished to stay for a month or more and the ultimate were elite condos for the whales, the very high rollers with millions of dollars to spend on their every whim. The flyer didn't have a minimum fee for the condos, it just had 'negotiable' instead.

On the right side was the casino. It was so huge, I couldn't see all of it without walking for almost twenty minutes. All the lights were off except for the security lighting which gave the room a ghostly appearance. We decided to split up and walk down different pathways from one side of the casino to the other.

It was kind of spooky without the bells, whistles and flashing lights but we didn't see anything out of the ordinary.

We moved on to the restaurants and bars, all very plush, no Johnny Rocket franchise to be seen, no Starbucks either. However, it was all pretty ordinary…ordinary opulence.

We checked out a few of the hotel rooms, randomly selecting a variety of accommodations. Same o, same o. We moved on to the condos, some of which were, in my opinion, ridiculously large. I mean, who needs five bathrooms?

The nightclubs were next on the list. The first four were routine, the last one had six brass poles and a VIP section. The sign over the entrance wasn't turned on but I could still read it: **Dolly's Hide Out.** This must have been a spin off from the place that gave Beaner his T-shirt. There were full size pictures of beautiful women dressed in a smile adorning every wall. I thought I was going to have to drag Clyde out of there, he'd drooled all over his shirt.

It was getting late as we entered the last place on our list: **Sodom and Gomorrah.** It was huge. I estimated it covered a whole acre on its own. It was located on the northeast corner of the outer wall and divided into two sections. We entered through another set of double doors into a spacious lobby. There was still about an hour before the sun set and light from the two large skylights provided illumination for the entire lobby. There was a fountain in the middle of the room and several marble statues, all nude of course, in what could be called provocative poses. To the left, was a hallway with the name Sodom above the hallway entrance. On the right was an identical hallway with the name Gomorrah placed above the entrance.

At the very back of the lobby was a large door. Actually, it looked more like a bank vault than a door. A sign on the door read **Private. Do Not Enter.** As if anyone but a safe cracker could open it.

I went down the hallway to Sodom with Bear. Sheriff Jones took the Gomorrah side with Clyde. Jerry decided to stay in the lobby with the nude statues.

There were three or four rooms on the Sodom side. The first one was named Orgy. The room was pitch black with only the light from the security lights shining through the opened door. I turned on my flashlight as I stood in the doorway and did a quick scan of the room. It was a very large room with what looked like a very large circular pool in the center. There was a carpeted path that led from the door to the pool. Just as I was about to walk to the pool, Bear found the light switch on the wall next to the door.

There were actually four switches, one was a rheostat which he slid upward, bringing up the indirect lighting that circled the room. He turned on another switch and the pool area lit up with what would be underwater lights, except there wasn't any water. And it wasn't a pool, it was a gigantic hot tub.

Between the wall and the hot tub, built in mattresses took up most of the room except for the paths that led to two bars on opposite sides of the room. One was named Alcohol and it was well stocked with everything from every brand of beer I could think of to 151 Bacardi, 190 proof vodka and of course champagne at a thousand dollars a pop. A sign on the bar read **For a New Treat, Try Our Moose River Hummer.**

The other bar was named Drugs. They offered everything from pot in various forms all the way to opium pipes and injectable heroin. A sign over the bar read **Patrons are NOT Allowed to OD.** Each bar was well stocked with a large variety of condoms, vibrators and butt plugs.

I'd seen enough, actually more than I ever wanted to see. We left and moved down the hall to the next room named Gays. I opened the door and saw beds, showers and hot tubs and a substantial variety of pictures showing intimate scenes of same-sex coupling. So on to the third room.

This room was named S & M. I opened the door, turned on the light, scanned the room and saw chains, handcuffs, whips and other torture devices. I shut off the light and headed to room number four. This room was named Pedophiles. I stood at the door, unable to reach for the knob. Bear put his hand on my shoulder and said, "Let me take a quick look, boss. No need for you to see this place."

He opened the door, turned on the light, scanned the room for five seconds, then turned off the light and closed the door. "I can't believe people can do that sort of thing to children. They're worse than animals. The Choctaw killed anyone who messed with children. No trial, just a lot of women with clubs and knives. When they were done, you wouldn't know it had been a human being, just a pile of blood, guts and bones."

I looked at him as we turned and walked toward the lobby. "That's a tradition I hardily endorse," I replied.

Sheriff Jones and Clyde had already returned to the lobby and were waiting for us. I asked, "What did you find?"

"We found that there are too many perverts in this world," the Sheriff answered. "Seeing all this made me feel dirty, really dirty. Let's get out of here, I need a shower."

The sun had set and there was little light in the lobby as we turned to leave. We stopped when we heard the vault door begin to open. The sheriff and I turned quickly drawing our weapons as the light from inside the vault spilled out flooding the lobby with bright white light.

A woman came out the vault and said, "Hi guys. I'm Dolly, owner of Dolly's Hide Out. How y'all doin'?" She saw our weapons and raised her hands in mock surprise. "Whoa, I surrender," she laughed. "You must be part of the new security team."

Before anyone could say a word, I said, "You're right. We're part of the new security. How did you get into the vault?"

Her expression changed to puzzlement. "Through the back door. How did y'all get in?"

"We came up the main road and entered through the lobby. Nobody told us about a back door," I replied.

"You're kidding, right? Did they forget to tell you about the ruling council meeting too?"

As Davy and I holstered our weapons, I said, "Sorry, miss…what should I call you?"

"Call me Miss Dolly, big guy. What's your name? Are you the leader?"

"No ma'am, I'm just one of the grunts. You can call me Joshua. Our leader must have been delayed. Maybe you could give us the tour of the vault and tell us about this meeting just in case our leader doesn't show up in time."

"Of course, Josh. Come on in and I'll show you around and introduce you to my girls."

She turned and led us into the vault where the lighting was…kind of like the lighting for a board meeting, somewhat bright. It was certainly bright enough for us to see what a beautiful woman Dolly was. She had a perfect figure and wore clothes that, to my way of thinking, were a little racy for a business meeting. Her makeup was also better suited for a cocktail party rather than a work meeting. I asked her, "Are you part of the ruling council, Miss Dolly?"

"What?! Me part of the council? Hell no! Me and my girls are the entertainment after the meeting is over. During the meetings we serve the high mucky mucks drinks and food and smile and look pretty. Speaking of my girls," she turned and yelled in the direction of a side door, "come on out girls, I've got some dudes who are dying to meet you."

I heard several girls began giggling as the door opened to what must have been a dressing room and seven stunningly beautiful girls walked out dressed in tight fitting T-shirts with Dolly's Hide Out written across the front, colorful thongs with sparkling sequins and very high heel shoes. I heard Jerry say in a hoarse whisper, "Oh, my lord! We must have died and gone to heaven."

Apparently, Dolly must have heard. She looked first at Jerry then at Clyde. "Don't I know you two boys. You look very familiar to me. Didn't you come visit my place in Tupelo?"

Apparently, Jerry had become tongue-tied, so Clyde answered for them both. "Yes, Miss Dolly, we're regular customers."

Doll's expression changed to one of doubt. "How did you two boys become security guards? You don't fit my idea of a guard."

Jerry found his voice and answered. "We were hired as temps until they could get some real guards. Ain't that right, Clyde? These other three are some of the new guards."

"What happened to the old guards? They used to be regulars as well. I haven't seen them in a while," she asked.

I answered, "They met with misfortune and won't be returning. We were told the resort would be opening soon. They're recruiting a lot more men and women to provide a safe environment for all our guests. I'm told they are looking at ex-military and police, all with combat experience."

Changing topics, Davy asked, "Could you show us the backdoor entrance? It would sure speed things up compared to walking through the whole resort to get to here."

Dolly thought for a moment before answering, then said, "Since we're working for the same bosses, I guess it would be alright. But the two temps have to stay here."

She gestured to her girls and said, "Keep our friends entertained until I get back." Then she turned back to Davy, Bear and me and said, "Come on, gentlemen."

She opened another door which led to an extensive kitchen and pantry area. There was a narrow walkway to the back wall with a wide rollup door. She pushed a button on a switch next to the door and it began to roll up. "This is where they deliver supplies to the vault kitchen but it's also where me and the girls enter for these ruling council meetings. The council members come in the same way or through the vault door if they have been somewhere inside the resort. They provided me with a remote that I must keep on me at all times. They change the code periodically. As you can see there's a small parking lot and a ramp where the trucks backup to unload. There is a separate road off SR 370 that leads to this back entrance. The back of this building is really part of the ten-foot wall that surrounds the resort."

She pushed a button on the remote and the door rolled down and locked. When we got back to the conference room Clyde and Jerry each had one of the girls sitting on their laps. Clyde stood up quickly dumping the girl onto the floor. Jerry had his arms wrapped around his girl like he was never going to let her go. We ignored them and Bear asked Dolly, "Who are the members of the ruling council? We'd like to know who we will be protecting."

Dolly hesitated, deciding what she could tell us and not get in trouble. "Let's move to the other end of the table and leave your two love birds to their passions." The conference table was long, capable of seating up to twenty people. There were nine chairs on each side and one at each end. Dolly sat at the end and we took seats close to her, (really comfortable chairs, by the way). "Okay, first of all please don't tell anyone I told you this. I really want to help you out but some of these guys are ruthless and would kill me if they found out I had identified them, even if you're security."

Davy said in a soothing voice, "We understand. We don't want you to get in trouble, just tell us what you're comfortable with."

She reached out and patted Davy's hand, took a deep breath and let it out slowly. "Okay," she said. "First of all, I think there are a dozen of them. They all don't turn up for the meetings but there are never more than twelve. I don't know the names of everyone, some only by what they do. There are three crime bosses or cartel leaders, not sure exactly what they do but one of them is from Mexico or maybe South America. He's a very powerful drug lord.

One is from Russia, he has a very heavy Russian accent and a piercing stare that scares me every time he looks at me. The last one is from either Vegas or New York, maybe Atlantic City. All three of them are the main sponsors who paid for the construction of the resort."

Bear interrupted her, "How did you get all this detail on them. Were you at the table during the meeting?"

"Are you kidding!? No, I sat in a chair in a corner of the room. I was furniture, someone to yell at if they wanted another drink. After a while, it was as if I wasn't there. I never spoke unless one of them asked me a question or asked for a drink. I just sat quietly with a blank stare. These people are very scary.

"The people I do know are nowhere near as scary but they are powerful. There are two members of the Union County Board of Supervisors, Keith Lovett and George Bridges. Lovett is a pompous ass. He used to be a preacher but he's the biggest hypocrite I have ever had the displeasure of meeting. He used to come into my club and demand free lap dances. He said he needed to make sure the girls were following the rules of distance and contact with the customers. I had him thrown out of the VIP room for groping the dancers several times and finally told our bouncer he was black listed and not allowed in the club."

She turned to Bear and said, "One of them is a Choctaw chief from one of the southern reservations. Not sure of his name. It's Eagle something."

Bear nodded his head. "I know him. He already has a casino on his rez. He is a smart man and ruthless."

"Did y'all see the orientation show?"

We nodded and she said, "The man you saw in the orientation is general manager of the resort, owns a five percent interest and is a member of the ruling council. His name is George Ladue. Other than those people there are two lawyers, a man and a woman. I'm not sure of their names. The last one was the head of our security, Fred Womack. I heard he was recently killed."

She looked at her watch, frowned and said, "You guys need to go. The meeting is scheduled to start in about an hour and you're not on the attendance list. We need to get things set up. Stop by my club sometime, drinks and lap dances are on the house."

We had to pry the girls off of Clyde and Jerry before we began the long walk through the resort to the lobby and the limo. On the way, Davy asked me, "It sure would be nice if somebody had planted some bugs while we were inside the vault. We could hear what was going on, hear their plans and all."

I reached into my pocket and pulled out a handful for very tiny black box like objects. "You mean like this? I put ten of them all around the room and a couple of spy cams too."

"Aren't you afraid they'll sweep the room for bugs," asked Bear.

"Let them sweep all they want. These are new tech. They don't turn on unless someone is speaking. When it's quiet, they're just a tiny lump of black plastic.

We climbed in our limo and headed down the hill to the parking lot with the Sheriff driving again. About half way down Jerry was shot by a sniper. He was sitting in the back next to the door when the window exploded and the bullet hit him in the side of his head. Like the window, his head exploded covering the rest of us in his blood, bones and brains. Clyde was sitting next to Jerry when it happened and went crazy with fear. He began screaming, trying to move as far away from Jerry's body as he could.

The Sheriff floored the accelerator and began a high-speed random weaving pattern down the access road to make us a more difficult target. We slammed through the gate at the security stop, tore through the parking lot and screeched to a stop beside one of the large casino buses.

We left Jerry's body in the limo and managed to get to my truck. There were no more shots. They were just sending us a message.

CHAPTER 26

Battle Planning—Joshua

Sheriff Jones drove us directly to the Union County Sheriff's Office just outside of Jericho. We hustled Clyde out of the rental truck and into the office. Fortunately, it was a slow night and they had no prisoners in lock up. Davy told me where the showers were and I took Clyde to get cleaned up. He had finally quit screaming during the run from the limo to the pickup and now he was almost catatonic. I had to turn on the shower and push him inside, clothes and all. He just stood there as the hot water sprayed down on him, washing the remains of his friend down the drain.

I told him to take his clothes off, got no response. I had to step in and strip him. I threw his clothes into a nearby garbage can and got a bright orange prison jumpsuit from a deputy. When I returned, Clyde had turned off the water and was sitting on a bench inside the shower, shivering as tears ran down his face.

I threw him a towel and told him to dry off. He turned his head and stared at me as if I was speaking a different language. But after a moment, he nodded his head and began to dry himself. I handed him the jumpsuit and he slowly put it on.

While I was with Clyde, the sheriff was reporting the murder and sending deputies to the crime scene. He also called a friend who was a reporter for a local newspaper. It was a weekly paper but it was going to press later this evening. He promised her an exclusive, if she could get it into tomorrow's edition.

He was just finishing up with the reporter when Clyde and I came walking into the office area.

The sheriff looked at Clyde and shook his head. "You look terrible, Clyde. How are you doing?"

Clyde had managed to stop crying but speaking was too big a challenge. He just shrugged his shoulders and mumbled something we couldn't make out.

Bear was sitting on a bench in the outer office and got up and put his arm around Clyde and said to us, "I'll take care of him. I'm the one who got him to become a guard. I'll take responsibility for him."

Davy glanced at me and said, "For safety sake, I think we should all stay here tonight. This is the safest place I can think of and we're all potential targets. We have enough empty cells for us to use. What do you think, Joshua?"

I nodded my head. "Good idea, Sheriff. Do you have any meds that could help Clyde to sleep tonight?"

Before he could answer, Bear interrupted, "I have some Choctaw medicine. He will sleep well. I saw a cell with two cots. I will stay with Clyde tonight. Okay?"

"That works for me," replied the sheriff. "One question, Bear. Do I need to know what Choctaw medicine you're going to give him?"

"Best if you don't know, Sheriff. Good night." Bear turned and guided Clyde to the holding cells and had him lay down on one of the cots. He gave him something to swallow and a sip of water, then turned out the lights and made sure the cell door remained unlocked, just in case they needed to make a quick exit.

I turned back to the sheriff and said, "The vehicle impound yard is behind this station, isn't it?"

He nodded. "Yes, what do you need?"

"I need to spend the night inside my ride," I answered. "I have to report to my superiors what happened at the resort and the murder. I'll be able to listen in on the ruling council meeting. If we're lucky we might get some video too. Another plus is that my vehicle is almost impenetrable and it's equipped to return fire when needed. I can also sleep in it. The seats recline into a queen size bed."

"Wow. That doesn't sound like government issue." When I didn't reply, he asked, "Who are you? I know you're not a BIA agent. I have a cousin pretty high up in the chain of command and he's never heard of you and they have no record of authorizing an inspection of the resort. So, who is the real Joshua Brown and what is your mission here in Jericho?"

I stared at him for a minute, then answered. "Good police work, Sheriff Jones. I figured you'd check up on me. Let me ask you a question before I answer yours. Did you know, I had been fibbing to you before we drove up that hill to the resort?"

"Yes, but I think 'fib' is a little weak when we are discussing what you're really doing here."

I shrugged. "Possibly. Okay, Joshua Brown is my real name and I do work as a special agent for a government agency, an American government agency which I can't divulge to anyone without authority from my superiors. As far as my mission in Jericho, I'm authorized to prevent the opening of the resort by any and all means necessary. Deadly force is approved. Collateral damage is frowned upon."

The sheriff just stared at me for a moment, then asked, "Where are your supporting troops? When can we expect them?"

I smiled slightly and asked a question in return, "Are you familiar with the old saying, 'One riot, one ranger?' There's your answer Sheriff, all though I have requested two specialists to join me. They should be arriving tomorrow."

"So, you're cutting me out of the action? That's not going to happen, Joshua. The murder of Jerry is related and I need to be involved."

"Are you volunteering to take orders from me?" I asked.

"No, not if I have to break the law but I will seriously consider any suggestions you might have."

We stood there for a long minute staring at each other. Finally I said, "That works for me. Don't you have to get to your crime scene?"

"Leaving now," he said. "I'll take you out to your combat vehicle and check in with you when I get back."

I walked across the impound yard and pressed a button on my remote control. One button disarmed my antitheft device, unlocked all the doors and powered up everything except the diesel. If we had been riding in my vehicle coming down the hill from the resort, Jerry would still be alive. The armor plating and the specially treated windows would have stopped any bullet up to and including a fifty-caliber round. Not only that, my offensive electronics would have tract the incoming round to its origin and returned fire on the shooter. I decided I wouldn't get out of this machine until the mission is successfully completed or I need to take a leak.

I climbed inside and said, "Computer on. Contact Leader." Immediately, the screen lit up with the image of my boss.

There were no pleasantries, I gave him a very succinct briefing of our activity at the resort, including the loss of one of our good guys. I told him I would monitor the ruling council meeting which was scheduled to begin shortly and that I linked the signal to his com system so he could monitor the meeting in real time as well. That assumed the bugs and the video had not been discovered.

When I was done with my briefing, the boss told me he was sending me a link to a very interesting TV news program that just aired from a local channel in Memphis. Then he signed off.

I opened the link and hit play. The news anchor introduced the viewers to Mr. Holo (better known as George Ladue). The anchor sat facing the camera and said, "Today we have a guest with us who is going to give the people of southern Tennessee and northern Mississippi a long awaited message." The anchor turned to his left as the camera pulled back to include George and said, "With us today is Mr. George Ladue, general manager of the new resort located near Jericho. Good evening Mr. Ladue, what is your message?"

The camera dollied into a close-up of George who smiled and said, "Please Bill, call me George. And yes, the long wait is over. I'm happy to announce, our new resort hotel and casino will be opening next weekend, ten days from today. As everyone is aware, we have had some setbacks, specifically in the area of staffing but those issues have been resolved and we're ready to go live. Our gates will be opened at noon on Saturday."

As Mr. Holo, aka George Ladue, was talking, an aerial view of the resort was shown. It had to be from a drone because the point of view for the camera had descended to street level showing the fountain in the turnaround and panned to the entrance. Then it moved through the wide-opened doors into the lobby area showing the paintings, the marble columns and the statues. The view faded out and a close up of George took its place.

"I want the audience to remember, this is an adults only resort, please make other plans for your children. There is no day care facility on site.

"If you've been to Atlantic City or perhaps Las Vegas and think you've seen it all, you are sadly mistaken. I guarantee you will be able to see and do things you never thought possible. If you're disappointed with your first visit, we will cheerfully refund every penny of your money. That's how sure we are that if you're looking for adult entertainment, we will satisfy your every desire."

They chatted for a few more minutes before the interview ended. I was ready to exit the feed when anchor Bill said, "In a related story, one of the new resort's security guards was found brutally murdered this evening near the resort's parking lot. We'll have all the details after these important words from one of our sponsors."

I fast forwarded through not one but several commercials. When the commercials were finished, the weather man talked about the new storm brewing in the gulf and the possible path it might make once it comes inland. Then they showed several reports on local sports and the upcoming Mississippi versus Tennessee football game. Coaches from both schools were interviewed. Finally, after I had fast forwarded for roughly ten minutes, they got back to the murder.

A young woman was holding a microphone and standing about thirty feet from the limo where we had left it. The limo's back door was opened and two techs were pulling the body out of the back seat and placing it on a gurney. The county medical examiner briefly examined the body and watched as the techs lifted the gurney with Jerry's body into the back of the ME's Expedition.

With that going on in the background, the reporter was talking to Sheriff Davy Jones.

"What can you tell us about this murder? Are you sure it was a murder and not a horrible accident?"

The sheriff looked at her like she was a complete idiot. "I'm positive it was a murder," he replied. "He was shot through the head by a high-powered rifle as he was coming down from the resort. He was a member of the resort's security staff. As of now, we have no suspects for the murder and no motive."

The reporter had been looking at the sheriff with a blank expression. When he stopped talking, she asked, "Do you think it might have been an accidental shooting, a hunter firing his rifle at what he thought was a game animal?"

The sheriff had been shaking his head from the moment she opened her mouth. When she stopped talking, he said, "The murder victim wasn't shot with a hunting rifle. He was killed by a fifty-caliber rifle used by police SWAT teams, military snipers and assassins. And I find it highly unlikely anyone could mistake a limousine for a deer. That's all the questions I have time for, I have a murder investigation to run."

He started to walk away but turned back to the reporter. "One last comment. We have an open murder investigation here at the resort. If I were you, I'd think twice about coming here until we arrest the murderer. Y'all have a good evening."

Bless his pea pickin' heart, I thought to myself. *That's going to rile a few people. Good for him.*

Five minutes after closing the video link, my bugs started broadcasting the ruling council meeting. A few seconds later I had video to go with it.

"What I want to know is who is the idiot who ordered the hit on the security guard," he said with a heavy Spanish accent. "When I find out who it is, I'm going to kill him. With my own two hands, I'll strangle the bastard who has prevented us from opening up." The large Hispanic man, I assumed he was a cartel boss, looked around the room at the other council members, looking for somebody dumb enough to raise his hand. When nobody volunteered to die, he pulled out a pistol from a holster under his suit coat and slammed it down on the conference table. "I'm going to start killing people one by one until somebody tells me who is responsible." Someone, probably one of his assistants, whispered in his ear then stepped back as his boss began looking around the vault. "You're right, Miguel. The old county supervisor, what's his name again?"

Someone out of desire to continue living, shouted out, "Keith Lovett! He's not here tonight."

"It was him? He's the screw up? I want him found and brought here, right now." Three men left quickly through the back door as the cartel boss picked up his gun and shoved it back into his holster. He turned to Dolly and said, "Get me a drink, bitch. Be quick about it."

A large man with a heavy Slavic accent asked no one in particular, "Did you see the news out of Memphis? The local sheriff is telling people to stay away from the resort until the murderer is found. That could take months. We cannot afford a delay like that. Especially after the other delays. Losing the Vietnamese and our four mercenaries has already cost us a fortune. We need to find a scapegoat but it has to be someone not associated with us. If our county supervisor turns up dead, things will just get worse."

The Hispanic man barked out a vicious laugh. "When I am done with this *cabron,* no one will recognize him. But I think you're right. We need someone to blame and a believable story to go with it."

Mr. Holo spoke up, "I think we should get somebody we could tag as a religious fanatic, some bible thumper who's out to shut us down because we are tempting the good people of Mississippi into sinful lives or something like that."

Both the Hispanic and Slavic crime lords began nodding their heads. The Slav smiled and said, "I like this idea. I like it very much. How about you, Carlos?"

Carlos seemed lost in thought for a moment then said, "Yes, Ivan. I think that would work. The sooner we find our scapegoat the sooner we can open this resort. And an added plus to me is that I get to kill the pendejo supervisor."

A third man spoke up, this one was a flashy dresser with a New York accent. "What about our plans for the big casino on Choctaw Lake? This Jericho resort is supposed to be a proof of concept. If we succeed here, we're going to move forward on a much bigger scale. That's where all the big money will come from. Not here, this was just a test. How about it Chief, Is the Choctaw Nation going to be able to wait for everything to blow over?"

Before the Chief could answer, they heard screaming and yelling coming from behind the door to the kitchen. Guns were drawn and pointed at the door. Suddenly, the supervisor burst through the kitchen door as if he had been shot from a cannon. It ripped the door off its hinges with the supervisor landing on top.

His face was cut and bloody and his right arm appeared to have grown a second elbow. He was screaming in pain as he tried to straighten out his broken forearm.

One of Carlos' bodyguards poked his head through where the door used to be and said, "Sorry about the door, boss. He didn't want to come."

"How did you find him so quickly?" Carlos asked.

"He was getting out of his car in the back parking lot. When he saw us, he tried to run. We grabbed him, he resisted, We…overpowered him and brought him to you as you ordered."

Carlos smiled at Manuel, then turned to the supervisor whose screaming had turned to a whimper. "I didn't do it. I swear I didn't do it. Please, you have to believe me."

Carlos kneeled down next to the supervisor and said in a soft almost soothing voice, "I know you didn't do it. You're too much of a coward to kill a man. But you got someone to kill him for you. Isn't that right?"

Lovett's eyes seemed to dart around the room, looking for someone, anyone, who would help him but he realized no one would come to his aid. His voice was a raspy whisper when he said, "Yes, I talked to a man I know. His name is Bart. He used to come to my church years ago. He was always bragging about how great a marksman he was during the war, claimed he could shoot the beak off a sparrow at three hundred yards. He even showed me his collection of sniper rifles. He'd had several run ins with our sheriff and told me he hated him. I also hated the sheriff. I knew he was going to be a problem for us, so I paid Bart to kill him. I told him the sheriff was at the resort and I'd give him another hundred if he killed him today."

"But the sheriff isn't dead, Bart killed the wrong man!"

"I know," whispered Lovett as a pain spasm came over him. "I guess he lied about how good he could shoot."

Carlos stood up, pulled his Smith and Wesson from his holster and shot Lovett twice.

The noise from the gun fire was deafening. For a moment, I lost audio. The first sounds I could hear was the voices of several women screaming, followed by the voice of Carlos, "Shut those crazy bitches up!"

The screaming stopped abruptly as I heard Carlos give commands to his guards, "Get this piece of shit out of here."

"What should we do with the body?" one of the guards asked.

"Take him outside and bury him!" Carlos yelled back. "The whole resort is built on top of a massive grave yard. No one's going to notice one more grave."

One of the video pickups showed two of the men bending down to pick up the body but one of them stood abruptly. "Boss, we got problems. This place is bugged!"

He reached under the conference table and pulled off one of my transmitters. Carlos said, "That's impossible. We swept the room before the meeting started. It was clean!"

Everyone came over to look at the small black box resting in the guard's hand. The Chief walked around the conference table with his hand brushing the underside. After walking a few feet, he stopped, leaned down, then reached under the table and pulled a second bug off. He stood raising his hand, showing the bug to the others. "Here's another one. Meeting's over. We need to get out of here…now!"

I'd placed another vid cam outside over the roll up door where it wouldn't be noticed. It recorded the license plate numbers of each of the cars as they left the parking lot. Two of Carlos' men dragged the body of the supervisor a few yards off the asphalt of the parking area, got shovels out of the back of their SUV and dug him a shallow grave. They threw the body in, covered it with dirt and drove away.

I got their license plate number too, as well as the location of the grave site.

Later that night, my two guests arrived, actually three guests if you include Sarge. The sheriff joined me in my war wagon (I really liked that name) as I drove to Memphis to pick them up. I filled them in on what happened at the vault during the ruling council meeting and how I thought we should move forward. On the drive back, I laid out what I wanted each of them to do.

I pulled the war wagon into the impound yard and stopped close to the sheriff's office. Everyone climbed out and headed inside except for Mark Riley and his partner, Sarge.

"I want Sarge to search the yard for hostiles and then stand guard at the back door," said Mark. "If that's okay with you, Sheriff?"

Davy nodded his approval and replied, "Good idea, Mark. Things are getting really dicey. I welcome the extra security."

Mark stayed outside as Sarge made his search of the impound yard. After the sheriff got Pham Bin Minh settled in his jail cell, Davy and I decided to step outside and see how Sarge performed. He ran to every car in the yard and did a quick pass around them. Every once in a while, he would sit briefly next to a car and bark. Sometimes he would bark once, other times, twice. He finished his rounds in less than fifteen minutes and returned to us at the back door.

Mark gave him a treat for his efforts and patted him on the head. "Good dog, Sarge. Another mission accomplished." Then he turned to the sheriff and said, "Sarge wants you to know you have four cars in the yard with drugs and two with explosives. That's what his barks were for."

The sheriff and I exchanged looks of surprise. "I'll be damned," exclaimed the sheriff. "That's incredible."

The sheriff had two of his deputies check out the suspect cars and everyone turned in for the night. Pham, Mark and Sheriff

Jones bunked in the jail cells while I returned to the comfort of my war wagon.

I awoke early the next morning to the sound of my phone buzzing in my ear. It was Dolly and she was pissed. "Did you plant the bugs in the vault, you son of a bitch!? You almost got me killed! Carlos is on a rampage. That bastard is paranoid and you just punched his insanity button!"

When she stopped for a breath, I said in a sleepy voice, "Good morning, Dolly. How's your day going? By the way, how did you get this number?"

"Answer me, damn it!" she screamed. "Did you plant the bugs?"

"Did you see me or anyone of my people plant any bugs? Maybe one of your girls planted them or maybe the people who brought in the vault's food and drinks did it."

"That's bull shit and you know it. I should have known better than to have told you anything about the vault."

"Did you tell anyone about us being in the vault?"

"Of course not. I'm not that stupid. Carlos or Ivan would have killed me on the spot if they ever found out about you."

"Did he question you?" I asked. There was a long pause, so I asked again, "Dolly, did he question you?"

"Yes," she finally answered, "He came to my club in Tupelo later that night, shut us down and kicked out everyone except me and my girls. Then he questioned me and all the girls."

I waited for her to say more, but she didn't. After a few minutes of silence, I asked, "Did he hurt you? Did he hurt any of the girls?"

I thought I heard a sob before she answered, "Of course he hurt us. That's his style. He said he would kill us all if we didn't tell the truth but after we saw what he'd done to the supervisor, none of us said anything. Two of my girls ended up in the hospital last night and I need about a week for my cuts and bruises to heal before I show my face in public."

I started to speak but she interrupted me, "I'm done. George called me this morning and said they had removed all the bugs and a couple of vid cams from the vault. He said Carlos had calmed down and he wants to have another meeting in the Vault at midnight, two days from now. I'd told him me and the girls would be there but I'm done. I thought this resort was going to make me a rich woman. It turns out, my greed nearly got me and a lot of my girls killed. I'm closing the club in Tupelo and leaving Mississippi for good. Going to change my name and get a job somewhere far from Carlos and the rest of them."

I started to say something but she interrupted me again. "Those people ruined my life. I wish…no, I pray somebody would kill all those assholes."

I answered, "Somebody will, Dolly. Soon, very soon," but she'd already hung up.

I sat in the war wagon for a few minutes to decide on our battle plan. When I was satisfied, I grabbed a small go-bag out of my duffle and headed for the back door to the sheriff's office. Sarge was fully awake, standing by the door wagging his tail. I took that as a good sign. He followed me in and went to the cell where Mark was sleeping and licked him awake. As I walked to the restroom to take care of business, I heard a groggy Mark say, "At ease, Sarge. I'm awake."

When I finished my business, I bumped into Mark on my way to the coffee machine. Bear and Davy were already in the break room and I joined them. There were too boxes of donuts sitting on the table. I took two chocolate iced cakes as I sat down. Between bites of my donuts and sips of coffee, I told them about the call from Dolly. By the time I was done, Pham, Mark and Sarge joined us and helped themselves to the donuts. Apparently, Sarge liked donuts too and placed his massive head on Mark's thigh and began whining like a small child. Mark fed him bites of plain cake donuts while I went over the battle plan.

For the next two hours, I presented the plan. I went through the details of each person's assignment. There was a lot of discussions and some excellent suggestions on how the plan could be improved. A general once told me, "If you want to accomplish a mission, listen to your specialists when you make your plans. They will know a hell of a lot more than you do about their area of expertise. Your job as leader is to integrate their suggestions into a workable plan."

When we came to an agreement on our course of action, I summarized, "Zero hour is 0000 hours two day from now. That would be midnight for you non-military people. We all have a lot to do before then, so let's get with it."

Pham contacted the Mississippi attorney general to file numerous criminal charges. Bear went back to the rez to have a private meeting with the chief. Sheriff Jones and a couple of his deputies headed up to the back door of the resort to dig up the remains of county supervisor Keith Lovett, establish a crime scene and speak with his reporter friend. Mark and I began the fabrication of numerous IEDs. In the early afternoon, after the sheriff and his people had left the crime scene, we took the war wagon to the resort's front parking lot. We unloaded seven of the drones and made several circuits around the outer wall mapping the best locations to place the IEDs

When we were done, we headed back to finish our bomb building. As we rolled out of the resort parking lot, I turned on my monitor to the local news channel in Memphis. While I drove, I had Mark check for news of the murder of the supervisor. He watched the sports news followed by the weather forecast that talked about the big storm moving into Mississippi, then, something unexpected. The news anchor said, "A man named Bart Evans turned himself in today at the Union County Sheriff's Office and admitted to killing not one but two men on the grounds of the new resort. When asked why he killed the two men, he said 'God told me to kill the evil perverts who were trying to bring more evil people to Jericho.' Sheriff Davy Jones confirmed the second death and that an investigation into the two murders was still ongoing and couldn't reveal any additional information at this time. On a side note, the new name for the resort has been made: The Jericho Resort and Casino."

By the next day, everything was set. The night before, the IEDs were placed in position. All we had to do was wait until midnight. Dolly's prayer would be answered.

CHAPTER 27

The Battle of Jericho--Joshua

At first light, the morning of the planned attack, I drove the war wagon to the parking area in the rear of the Jericho Resort Hotel and Casino. Traffic had been light and I planned to stay only a few minutes to launch the surveillance drone. This was a little bigger bird with a much longer battery life. It cost more than the cheap models we used to check out the resort wall but it was well worth the extra cash. This new one could stay aloft for at least a full day. It could also transmit live images as far away as the sheriff's office impound yard. Of course, those images were also being recorded to be used as evidence of what was to transpire later this evening.

I unfolded the drone arms, powered it up and launched it. The bird quickly climbed to its programmed altitude of three hundred feet and began to hover. Using my iPad, I positioned it so the camera focused in on the rear parking area, centered on the vault's back door. The resolution was so good, I could make out the small camera I had placed above the rollup door. I used the controls on my iPad to switch from the drone view to the view from the door camera to see if it was still active. The screen changed and I could now see my war wagon with me standing in front of it. I waved to myself and my image waved back. Very cool.

I locked in the settings on the surveillance drone, climbed into the war wagon and drove back to the impound yard just in time for new boxes of donuts. Sarge was there to greet me as I parked and he followed close behind me into the station.

"Good morning, boss," Davy said as I checked the opened donut box. Everyone was sitting at the table chowing down. Even Clyde was there with three donuts sitting on a napkin in front of him.

"Good morning troops," I said to them all. "Good to see you up this morning, Clyde. How are you doing?"

Clyde looked up at me as he stuffed half a donut into his mouth and took a sip of coffee. He said something as he chewed but all I could make out was, "…no dinner…hungry."

I sat down with my coffee and two chocolate frosted, chocolate cake donuts, did I mention they were my favorite? Sarge wedged himself between me and Mark, laid his head on the table eyeing the donut box and began making little whimpering sounds. To me, it sounded like he was dying from lack of food and apparently Mark agreed. He took a plain cake donut out of the box and began to break it in half but Sarge lunged at it and swallowed the whole donut in one bite. Mark quickly pulled back his hand and yelped, "Damn Sarge, don't eat the fingers." Satisfied, the dog licked his master's fingers as a gesture of apology and went to lie down next to the back door.

When the sheriff had finished eating, he asked me, "We gave our prisoner a big breakfast from McDonald's just before you came in. I'll give him a few more minutes before I begin interrogating him. Want to come along?"

Before I could answer, Clyde said, "I want to come too, sheriff." His voice was low and angry.

Davy shook his head. "Sorry, Clyde, as much as I would like to turn you loose on him for a few minutes, I can't let you near him. At least not for a while."

Clyde hung his head and took another donut from the box. The sheriff looked at me again and I said, "Yeah, I'll join you. Can I bring my iPad? Maybe it'll change his plea when he sees the Vault video."

We walked down the short hallway to the station's only interrogation room and waited for one of the deputies to bring in Bart Evans. Five minutes later there was a rap on the door and the voice of the deputy, "I got your prisoner, sheriff. He finished his breakfast and used the head."

"Bring him in," replied Davy.

The door opened and the deputy escorted the prisoner to a chair across the table from us. He sat down and the deputy attached his handcuff to a heavy-duty ring in the center of the table. The whole time, Bart never looked at either of us.

After the deputy left, Sheriff Jones said, "This conversation is being recorded and can be used as evidence in any court cases that follow. You understand me, Bart?"

Bart nodded his head and studied the metal ring in the middle of the table. "Say yes or no, Bart," said the sheriff.

Bart flashed up to look at the sheriff for an instance as he said, "Yes. I understand." Then he looked away.

The sheriff continued, "Yesterday, you came into this office and confessed to a deputy you were the man who shot and killed Jerry Graham and later that evening shot and killed county supervisor, Keith Lovett. Is that right? Bart."

Still looking down, Bart replied, "That's right, I done shot and killed 'em both. Shot 'em with my favorite sniper rifle. Lock me up. I'm guilty."

The sheriff sat quietly for a several minutes, letting the tension build, then said, "Look at me, Bart." The prisoner never moved, his head still bowed. Davy waited a moment then slammed the palm of his hand down on the table and shouted, "LOOK AT ME!"

Bart's head snapped up, a look of fear on his face. In a stern voice, the sheriff continued, "We both know you're lying, Bart. Even this gentleman sitting next to me knows you're lying. We know you killed Jerry Graham but you were supposed to kill me. You missed me and killed Jerry, blew his whole head off, blew his brains all over Clyde sitting next to him. Why did you do that? You knew both

Jerry and Clyde, I thought you were friends. But the real question is why did you want to kill me? Who paid you to kill me?"

Bart sat there, frozen in fear.

After the sheriff waited for a moment, he said, "That's okay, Bart. We already know who paid you. It was county supervisor, Keith Lovett. Wasn't it, Bart?"

Bart began to look confused; he began to nod his head, "How do you know? How could you possibly know?"

"We know it all, Bart. We also know you didn't kill the supervisor. Somebody else did and got you to say you did it. Did they pay you to say you killed him? Did they, Bart?"

As if in a trance, Bart began to babble, "It was some cartel boss, Carlos somethin'. He didn't pay me nothin'. He threatened to kill me and my whole family if I didn't confess. He said he'd make me watch him kill my wife and my kids, then he'd kill me." He was crying now, almost howling in pain.

"Okay Bart, we're done for now. I'm going to have a deputy take you back to your cell," said Davy as he pushed a call button for the deputy. As the deputy began undoing his cuffs from the table ring, Bart asked, "What's going to happen to me and my family now that you know?"

The sheriff answered, "We're going to protect your family from Carlos. He won't kill you either but you did kill Jerry. You're going to have to go to prison but at least you'll be alive."

As we walked out to the office area, Pham was just returning from his trip to Jackson, the capital of Mississippi. I asked him how it went. "Great," he replied. "We got all the warrants we requested. We can arrest all the ruling council members, provided they are alive after what you have planned tonight. Are you sure they are going to be in the Vault? I know what Dolly told you but I can't believe they would return to a place they know was already breached. I'd think they'd be more cautious than that."

"You could be right Pham," I replied. "This could be a trap. I think there's a fifty-fifty chance they'll be in the vault at midnight. It really doesn't matter to me. My mission is to prevent the resort from ever opening. If we get the scum bags who built it and plan to profit from it, that's just icing on the cake."

There was a sound of rumbling thunder as the lights in the office flickered briefly. We walked out the main entrance and looked up at the sky. Far to the south, large, black thunderheads covered the sky from horizon to horizon. Bear had joined us and Pham asked him, "What do you think, Bear? Is our game going to be rained out?"

The Choctaw looked at the sky and took a deep breath, then let it out slowly. "Maybe. Too soon to tell."

Clyde and the sheriff had also come outside to check the weather. Clyde looked at the darkening sky and said, "This game we're playing is more like football than baseball. Football games in Mississippi are never rained out."

We all turned and walked back inside.

I had a thought and turned to Clyde. "Do you have the number for Dolly's Hide Out?" I asked.

Clyde looked a little embarrassed as he pushed up his right sleeve. Tattooed on his forearm was a phone number. "My memory ain't too good, so I had it put where I could get to it in a hurry."

I called the number tattooed on Clyde's arm. It rang six times and then rolled to voice mail. It was a recording of Dolly's voice, "Hi, this is Dolly. I'm sorry to have to tell all my wonderful customers, we are going out of business. We're currently closed and will remain closed. Good luck on finding another place to hang out. Goodbye."

I walked outside and checked the weather again. The sun had gone down and it was pretty dark but it looked like it was getting worse. I decided I needed to address another option. I got into the war wagon and drove into Jericho to the Home Depot, found what I was looking for, then headed to the resort.

As I drove east on SR 370, I said, "Monitor on, access surveillance drone output." I pulled into the road leading to the vault's back door and parked in the lot. "Any contacts since launch?"

An electronic voice answered, "No contacts recorded." I started to get out of the car, but stopped when the monitor added, "Alert! Wind speed increasing. May not be able to maintain hover coordinates." I looked at the monitor and everything looked fine but as I watched, the picture seemed to shudder a bit. I shook my head. *This could become a serious problem,* I thought to myself.

Before I got out of my vehicle, I turned my three spotlights onto the top of the vault area. When I was satisfied I had enough light to work by, I got out of the war wagon, grabbed my extension ladder and the other hardware and walked towards the rollup door.

When I was done with my installations, I notice the wind was beginning to pick up and felt a few raindrops as I climbed down the ladder. I made a quick detour into the vault kitchen using my special remote to open and close the rollup door, then hurried to my ride. By the time I made it back to the sheriff's office, the rain had picked up. I had to turn on the wipers as I drove into town.

I parked the war wagon close to the back door. Sarge had been curled up on the door mat and stood to greet me. The bad weather didn't seem to bother him but he followed me inside as I met up with the rest of the crew. If he was looking for another donut he was out of luck, he'd have to wait until tomorrow like the rest of us. As I walked past the holding cells, I noticed Bart Evans was missing.

"What happened to Bart?" I asked as I walked into the office area.

Davy looked up from the TV and answered, "Federal Marshals picked him up and transported him to a secure location. They took his family too."

I noticed most of my crew was watching the weather channel and following the progress of the storm. Bear said, "I talked to my family on the rez. They say this is a very bad storm, strong winds and much lightning, heavy rain too."

Clyde added, "I heard a second storm from the Atlantic is merging with the one coming up from the Gulf. Do you think the ruling council will still meet with this weather?"

"That's not our top priority," I replied. "Our first objective is to keep the resort from opening. If the ruling council shows up, we arrest them if we can or take them out if we can't arrest them. If they don't show up, Pham has warrants for their arrests and we hunt them down."

I looked at the weather report and asked, "Any estimates on when the storms will hit Jericho?"

Davy answered, "The last I heard, sometime between 11:00 pm and midnight."

I checked my watch. It was almost 10:00pm. I wanted to be in position soon. I turned to the expectant faces and said, "It's time to gear up, full combat gear, automatic weapons as well as side arms. Davy, I think you should deputize all of the troops so we can make arrests if needed."

"Already done, Joshua, except for you."

"Thanks but as a special agent for the government, I can already arrest the bad guys."

Ten minutes later, we climbed into the war wagon and headed to the resort. It was only my troops involved. The regular deputies remained at the station to handle the normal business.

We took the turnoff to the back entrance and stopped. I checked the surveillance drone output. As of 10:30, there had been no contacts. Shortly after that we lost the drone signal.

I placed the war wagon in four-wheel drive mode running on electric motors. We turned off the road and turned away from the resort for about two miles, then turned ninety degrees and cruised as silently as we could until the GPS said we were directly in line with the vault door. At that point we slowly approached the vault until we were within five hundred yards of the resort wall. We went silent and dark and waited. There were only a few security lights on the top of the ten-foot wall but it made it easy to see. The rain was coming in strong gusts now and the lightning strikes were coming closer as the stormed moved toward the resort.

At 11:30, we saw the headlights of three limos moving up the road toward the rear entrance. They parked in the lot and it looked like maybe a dozen men got out and ran quickly into the vault to avoid the rain. "Check our six, Mark," I ordered quietly.

"Roger that," he replied. "Scanning…I've got six bogies, twenty yard splits, walking up slowly…They're well-armed…maybe two RPGs."

Meanwhile, the men who had entered the vault came running out with automatic weapons and took up positions behind the limos. They had us in a cross fire. We were set up.

"Mark, standby to detonate IEDs," I ordered.

"Ready to fire," he responded.

"Fire!"

The sky was illuminated as the several hundred IEDs which we made, detonated all at once. Even this far away from the resort, we could feel the concussion of the explosions. Once the roar of the bombs had ceased, we watched as section by section of the ten foot wall began to break apart, crumble and fall into the resort structures.

The men in the parking lot had been thrown to the ground by the explosions and were just now rising and running for their lives. I noticed at least two men had been crushed by some of the rubble from the wall.

The six men behind us had stopped moving forward momentarily but recovered quickly.

I punched the button on my weapons selector and activated the turret on the roof of the war wagon. The GE M134 mini machine gun mounted on the turret acquired the bogies and began spraying them at the rate of sixty rounds per second. Ten seconds later, all the bogies were down.

Mark opened the back hatch and he and Sarge jumped out. He took the dog's head in his hands and looking into his eyes, commanded, "Sarge, search and destroy." The dog turned and ran into the darkness.

A few seconds later, I saw a lone figure stand up about fifty yards from my side of the war wagon. He lifted the RPG to his shoulder and prepared to fire. I barely had enough time to yell, "Incoming RPG, nine o'clock," before he fired at us. The rocket struck the wagon in the middle of the body just below the window level and detonated with a deafening explosion. The enhanced armor prevented any penetration but the force of the explosion lifted us off the ground and flipped us on to the passenger side.

None of us were hurt, just stunned but I felt like a turtle lying on its back, in other words, pretty helpless. Then I heard the sound of automatic weapon fire coming from behind us. The hatch was still opened and I could see Mark lying on the ground, firing at the shooter.

Pham, Bear and Clyde had been sitting in the back when the RPG hit. They wasted no time exiting the vehicle by climbing over the seat and crawling out the opened hatch. Sheriff Jones, who had been sitting in the front passenger seat, climbed over two rows of seats and followed them. I cautiously opened my side door, slipped over the side and slid down the underside of the wagon looking for more shooters.

I heard Mark yell, "I got him, he's down."

I caught a glimpse of a large dog in body armor streaking toward where the shooter was down. A moment later, we all heard brief screaming and then silence. Mark was still on the ground when he said, "The shooter's dead now."

While all this was taking place, the storm had gotten worse but looking to the south, I could see the worst was yet to come.

We all got together and manage to push the war wagon back onto its four wheels and climbed inside. Mark remained in the back of the vehicle with the hatch opened while Sarge continued his search and destroy mission.

As I began a series of systems checks to see if we had lost any capabilities, I heard a distant sound, kind of like thunder but not quite. The wipers were still working and I could barely see the remnants of the wall we destroyed sliding down the hill. I lowered my window and listened. No, that wasn't what was making the sound. It was something else. What could it be? I was sure it wasn't thunder. But I couldn't figure out where the sound was coming from until Bear shouted, "We got company boss, I think it's more bad guys."

I popped up my radar tracker and prayed it still worked. We were in luck, bad luck. The radar identified nine vehicles. The radar analysis software suggested they were SUV size. They were four-wheeling through empty terrain coming straight at us.

"Any chance these are your reinforcements?" asked Davy. Before I could answer him, they started shooting at us. "I guess not," he said, answering his own question.

Mark jumped in the back and closed the hatch. Clyde shouted, "What about Sarge?"

Mark shouted back over the sound of the bullets pinging off our armor. "He'll be fine. He knows what to do."

While they were talking, I checked the mini machine gun. It was fine but we had limited rounds left. I chose the first two enemy SUVs and emptied my magazines on them. The lead vehicle exploded taking out another SUV in the process. The second target veered away and stopped. Steam was rising from under the hood. No one got out, I assumed they were KIA.

I quickly stowed the mini gun and brought up my rocket launcher. I had six rockets available and could fire two at a time. I locked the rockets' guidance systems on the next two SUVs and fired. I have to admit, when the rockets launch, they're pretty noisy and everybody hears as well as sees them coming at you but they're so damn fast you don't have time to get freaked out before you're dead.

We managed to take out five more targets with the rockets. That left two SUVs full of an unknown number of troops we would have to deal with. I had expended all the bells and whistles the war wagon had to offer. So, we were left to fight it out the old fashioned way. Not exactly hand-to-hand combat, at least not yet.

The two enemy SUVs stopped about fifty yards from us. They kept their headlights on high beam to illuminate us and blind us from their movements. Smart tactic, except we had two qualified marksmen, the sheriff and to my surprise, Clyde. They fired four quick rounds and took out all four headlights, leaving us in total darkness with howling wind, torrential rain, with a sound and light show thrown in for good measure.

I liked their idea of using the car headlights to blind us, so I thought I would play a little tit for tat. I turned on the war wagon's bright flood lights and lit them up. Before they could get behind cover I counted twelve people. Davy, Clyde and Bear took out three of them before they made it to cover. I heard one of their survivors yell in Spanish, *"Las luces, pendejos. Disparen a las luces."*

I recognized that voice. "Carlos, is that you? I know it is. You're under arrest for the murder of County Supervisor Keith Lovett and a lot of other things. By the way, our lights are covered with bullet proof glass. You got no chance of shooting them out. We'll just sit here and pick you off one-by-one."

My comment brought a flood of colorful Spanish profanity, ending with something about my mother, which was followed by a hail of gunfire. Pham was inside the war wagon monitoring the entire battle area and warned me, "Joshua, they're using the gunfire as a distraction so they can flank us. They have two going left and another two to the right, leaving five in front of you."

It couldn't have been more than a minute or two before I heard screaming coming from the left, followed by gun fire, more screaming, then only the sound of the storm.

I motioned to Bear and he met me behind the opened driver side door. "Are you a good tracker?" I asked.

He looked at me for a moment then said, "Of course, I'm Choctaw."

"There are two bad guys who're trying to flank us on the right. Can you find them and kill them quietly?"

He smiled. "Sure boss. Choctaws like killing white men, it's in our blood."

"How about Mexicans?"

"Close enough," he answered and quietly slipped into the darkness.

I turned back to Carlos and his four remaining mercs. "Why don't you surrender? You've lost almost all of your mercenaries. They must have been your new security people. The resort is done for. It will never be opened. You and your other investors have spent all that money for nothing. If you continue to fight, you'll die. If you surrender now, I'm sure your attorneys will find some sort of legal loophole that will get you off and back to Mexico where you belong."

For a moment, I thought he was considering surrendering. Wrong again.

"You stupid *gringo*. I am Colombian, not Mexican and I will not surrender…ever! I will not leave this battle field until I have your *cajones* to take with me. I will put them in my trophy box in my luxurious mansion in Bogota. Every time I look at them, all nasty and shriveled, I will laugh at your feeble attempt to challenge me."

And so it went, back and forth, until Bear appeared out of the darkness holding the scalps of the two mercenaries.

I turned back to Carlos just in time to hear a dull whump that sounded like a mortar. Everyone dove for cover but when it hit, there was no explosion, just the hissing sound as the sleeping gas spread across the ground. My last thought was, *This isn't supposed to happen. We're the good guys.*

I awoke to a flash of lightning and an explosion of thunder that seemed to last forever. A deluge of water was falling on my face and I thought I was being water boarded. I sat up abruptly and saw Carlos smiling down at me. My mind was foggy but I realized one of his men must have bound my hands behind my back with a zip tie.

Two mercs hauled me to my feet and I immediately threw up. The gas has that effect on me. Carlos said nothing at first, I took his silence as an opportunity to see how the rest of my troops were doing. Carlos laughed when he saw me looking at my friends. "They are still out. There is no one to help you. You're a dead man, actually, you're all dead men but first I must perform a small surgery on you." He motioned to the two mercs. "Remove his pants, underwear too."

One of the men grabbed me around the chest and the other knelt down and began to remove my pants. I did two things at once. Since my hands we're restrained behind me, I pushed myself back until I could feel his body against my back, then reached with my fingers and crushed his private parts with all the strength I could muster. At the same time, I brought up my right knee into the face of the man kneeling in front of me, breaking his nose and fracturing his jaw. Both men were screaming in pain as both fell to the ground. I quickly stepped forward and stomped on one man's windpipe then the other's and the screaming stopped.

The remaining two mercs were ready to shoot me but Carlos yelled at them to stop. "No, shooting him would be too easy a death for him. I want him to suffer. If he moves, shoot him in the leg."

As he walked toward me, he pulled a knife, a very large knife, from a sheath on his belt. He walked toward me, tossing the knife from one hand to another in the pouring rain. He circled to one side of me, then the other.

"Are we going to dance or are you going to start some serious cutting sometime this week?" I said taunting him to make a move but then it happened.

The lightning bolts were so bright anyone looking at them would be temporarily blinded. I was facing away from the lightning so I could see fine but the three of them stood there in blind shock as bolt after bolt of lightning rained down on the lightning rods I had placed on the roof of the vault and areas called Sodom and Gomorrah. I counted at least seven strikes followed by a massive explosion.

The lightning had ignited the gas that had filled the vault and the adjacent wings named for the evilest cities of the ancient world. I had turned on the stove's gas burner and disabled the lighter. The gas had been flooding the building for almost half a day. The explosion and the related fire would burn for days. Nothing would be left.

When the lightning stopped and Carlos and his men were able to see again. He was insane with rage. "KILL HIM! Kill him no…"

Before he could finish his order, a large, incredibly fast dog or perhaps a wolf, dressed in body armor came crashing through the men, knocking them to the ground and their weapons from their hands. Sarge slowly approached Carlos, with a deep throated growl. When Carlos lifted his knife, the dog lunged at him knocking him to the ground and then bit down hard on his crotch, shaking his head back and forth like a puppy with his toy. At first Carlos was screaming but soon passed out from the pain.

Sarge let go of Carlos and stared at the other two men. The dog began barking and they scrambled to their feet and ran off into the dark, rain-soaked field. He watched them go then turned and trotted over to me. I smiled at him and said, "What a good dog, Sarge. You saved my life and got rid of so many bad guys. You can have all the donuts you want."

He barked his agreement and left to go wake up Mark and the others.

When the others had regained consciousness, Bear cut off my zip ties and handed me my Desert Eagles. I walked over and looked down at Carlos. I couldn't tell if he was dead or not. I didn't care. I put two shots into his head, one for each eye. He would be a blind man in hell forever.

All of us stood leaning against the war wagon and watched the fire consume the resort. It would probably burn for days. The rain had stopped and the storm was moving slowly off to the north. We climbed into the war wagon and headed back to Jericho. As I drove, I mentally checked off my mission requirements. I concluded it had been a very successful mission. The battle of Jericho was over. Praise the Lord.

PART 4

CHAPTER 28

The Debriefing—Joshua Brown

A few days after the events which took place at the Jericho Resort Hotel and Casino, I received orders to come to Washington D.C. for a formal, face-to-face debriefing. My orders indicated I was supposed to drive my war wagon to Memphis where it would undergo a 'complete examination, repair and rearm.'

I would leave the war wagon in Memphis and fly by military aircraft to Andrews Air Force Base in Maryland, close to our nation's capital. I was to board my flight the next day at the Tennessee Air National Guard side of the Memphis International Airport.

I said my good-byes to Sheriff Davy Jones, Clyde and Bear and relayed a message from my boss that they would receive 'substantial compensation for their participation in the Jericho mission.' Of course, they were told to treat the details of the mission as classified and not to be shared with anyone. There followed some fancy legal words saying they would forfeit their 'substantial compensation' if they went blabbing to reporters or wrote a book on the details of the mission. If they sold the movie rights to some film producer, they would spend the rest of their lives in a federal prison.

Pham, Mark and my new best buddy, Sarge, rode with me to Memphis. I dropped them on the commercial side of the airport for their flight back to Portland. The powers-that-be pulled some strings to get Sarge on board the flight by supplying papers that he was a therapy dog. He got the window seat in first class with Mark on the aisle. Pham sat across the aisle. It was the first time any of them had flown first class.

After I dropped them off, I took the war wagon to a Memphis chop shop under contract to the government for the rework and upgrades. I took a cab from the chop shop to the Airport Hilton and spent the rest of my day polishing my After Action Report. I took all my meals in the hotel and didn't checkout until it was time to head to the Air National Guard Base.

Instead of the C-17 and its comfortable cabin area with first class seats, my ride was a C-130 turboprop with canvas fold down seats against the side of the fuselage. The seats faced inward so I got a great view of an armored personnel carrier along with a Marine company that was also hitching a ride to Andrews.

The flight took a little over an hour before we were back on the ground. I was met by a limo and whisked to a fancy hotel close to the White House. I was told the meeting would be tomorrow morning in a secured conference room at 1000 hours. Be prepared to spend the entire day in the meeting and don't forget to wear a suit and tie.

Later that day, I went to a very exclusive men's shop located in the hotel lobby area and bought my first suit since joining the Marines fifteen odd years ago. I also picked up two dress shirts, three ties and a pair of shoes, socks and a belt. I got a shave and a haircut in the hotel barber shop, a manicure and a massage. I billed it all on my government credit card.

I was up at 0600 hours the next morning and had room service bring my breakfast. I went to the hotel fitness center for an hour, came back to my room, showered and put on my new suit. At 0945 hours, there was a knock at my door. A Marine in his dress uniform escorted me to the secure conference room. Promptly at 1000 hours, I rapped on the door three times.

"Come," said a voice from the other side and I entered the room.

I stepped inside, came to attention and announced myself. "Special Agent Joshua Brown, reporting as ordered."

The room was dark except for one chair illuminated by an overhead light shining straight down from the ceiling. "Please take a seat, Special Agent," said a detached voice.

As I crossed the room to the chair, I began to feel somewhat uncomfortable. The set up reminded me of a movie where several Nazis were interrogating a Jewish spy.

I sat down, placed my iPad on the table and waited. I tried to see if there was anyone sitting across from me but it was just too dark.

A woman was first to speak. "We apologize for these precautions but it would be best if you couldn't identify us. In a government with many secrets, our organization is at the top of the list. Very few people even know we exist. In the past you had one point of contact, a man you sometimes refer to as The Leader. That is changing for reasons we will explain later. First of all, we need to ask you a few questions regarding your last mission."

A man's voice spoke up, a voice I didn't recognize, not my leader's voice. "We all have followed your activities from Nogales to Portland and finally at Jericho. You submitted your plan for carrying out your three missions but never followed any of your plans. Why is that?"

I asked a question in return. "Were you ever in the military, sir? Any of the services?"

There was a pause, then the same voice said, "Why do you ask?"

"Your last question makes me think you are a politician, always answer a question with another question. The reason I asked is that anyone with any military experience knows their best initial plans go out the window ten minutes after a conflict begins. You can always assume you know how your enemy will react but in most cases, you need to be able to improvise and use whatever the situation calls for. Does that answer your question sir?"

There was silence, then a different woman asked, "Why did you shoot Carlos in the eyes? Don't you think that was overkill?"

"No ma'am, I don't," I replied. "He was going to have me killed and would have succeeded if it wasn't for a Marine dog. He was badly injured by the dog who saved my life. Carlos would probably have bled out from his wounds but he had caused the death of many people and I didn't want him to recover and have some high-priced lawyer keep him from getting the death penalty. So I killed him. I shot him in both eyes to keep him from being mostly dead. I wanted him completely dead."

Another man interrupted and said, "Who made you judge, jury and executioner?" His voice was full of indignation.

"Why, you did. I was given the authority to do what I thought needed to be done. When I took this position, I asked my leader what my rules of engagement entailed. He told me, I wasn't limited in my actions. He told me I should think of myself as the Angel of Death. I don't kill good people, I protect them from wicked, evil people. I always give the wicked ones an opportunity to change their evil ways. Unfortunately, wicked people don't want to stop being evil. So I kill them and I do it in such a way as to discourage others from becoming evil."

Another male voice changed the direction of the questions. "How did you know placing lightning rods on the roof of the vault and the adjoining Sodom and Gomorrah rooms would result in their total destruction?"

"I didn't know it would. I thought it was a long shot but worth the small amount of effort in case the storm would arrive over the resort." I thought for a minute then added, "There were numerous unknowns going into the battle. The Ruling Council could have shown up and we would have still blown the IEDs and destroyed a substantial amount of the resort but I knew that might not happen. So I planned for every contingency I could think of. Unfortunately, I didn't think of the mortar with the sleeping gas. It almost cost me and my troops our lives. If It hadn't been for Sarge, we'd all be dead and Carlos and his buddies would be planning how to open the resort."

"I have a technical question I'd like to ask," came a voice out of the dark I hadn't heard before. "It's my understanding lightning rods are placed on buildings to prevent the very thing that happened at Sodom and Gomorrah. Why did those buildings explode when the lightning struck the rods?"

I smiled at that one. I had been waiting for it. "Lightning rods are designed to attract lightning bolts, to keep the lightning from damaging the house or building. In order for that to happen, the rod is attached to a copper wire or cable which runs down the side of the building and is usually connected to an underground water line. The energy of the lighting is diverted from the building and runs down the copper line and disperses into the ground. In the case of the resort, I attached seven lightning rods to the roofs of the buildings without grounding them. All of the energy of the lightning exploded into the buildings, blowing them apart. It also caused the gas from the Vault kitchen stove to explode, resulting in the total destruction of most of the buildings in that area."

Another woman asked, "How did you know the storm would be centered over that particular place at that exact moment?"

"Obviously, I didn't know. When I bought the lightning rods at Home Depot, there were only light showers in our area. The forecast said the storm was supposed to hit Jericho sometime between 11:00 pm and midnight. That's all I knew."

One of the men asked, "So it was just dumb luck that led to the success of your mission?"

I waited to respond to his question. I needed to word it carefully. "I don't believe in luck, dumb or smart. I believe in being prepared for as many contingencies I can think of. As I mentioned before, I hadn't been prepared for the sleeping gas and it almost cost me my life."

Another voice, I couldn't tell if it were a man or woman speaking, replied, "But you didn't die. At the last second you were saved by a dog and a thunderstorm. Tell me, Special Agent Brown, do you believe in divine intervention?"

Before I could answer, one of the men said angrily, "Oh for crying out loud, how can you poss…"

He was cut off by my leader, "That's enough questions. I want to move on to our review of the three missions."

"Boss," I interrupted, "I'd like to answer the last question. I absolutely believe in divine intervention. I can't remember how many times I have been in near-death situations and walked away with very little damage, while everyone around me was either killed or maimed. I have no idea why I survived. Perhaps I've been chosen for these missions. I never take it for granted I will always be saved by some miracle, I always do my best to plan my missions for success but when things go wrong, as they sometimes do, I have succeeded."

The next couple of hours were spent reviewing the details of my AARs for my three missions. When it was finally over, my boss dismissed the rest of the group. No one said a word to me in parting, nothing, not even a good-bye or good luck on your future missions, or even you're such a schmuck.

In closing, the boss said, "I'll speak for the entire committee. I will remain your primary contact, at least for the foreseeable future. I will provide you with your mission orders and be your contact for any support. For the next month you will stand down. You're on leave and I want you to be on R&R for that entire time. Go visit friends and family, take a cruise or go fishing, whatever you want. Be sure to put it all on the government credit card. The only limitation is that you remain reachable in case an emergency comes up, understood?"

I nodded. "Thanks boss. Can I stay in the hotel for a few days? I'd like to take a tour of the area. I never had the chance before."

"Absolutely, stay as long as you want. In closing, I feel obligated to say you were a test case and you passed with flying colors. As a result, we will be bringing more people like you onboard in the near future. Now go enjoy yourself. You're dismissed."

CHAPTER 29

Epilogue

I walked back to my room, out of habit, periodically checking my six for threats. When I arrived at my door, I checked the tells I had placed between the door and the jam. They were still in place. I walked into my room and swept it for bugs, there were none so I turned on my jammer, checked the clothes closet and the shower and finally relaxed.

I removed my shoes and socks, took off my monkey suit and carefully hung it in the closet, followed by the tie and my dress shirt. I opened the safe in the closet and removed my two Desert Eagles and placed one under my pillow and the other on the nightstand. Dressed only in my skivvies, I walked to the large window and looked out at the city. There was a good view of the Potomac River and I could see a small part of the Arlington National Cemetery, the place where my twin brother, Caleb, was buried.

I must have stood there for a long time, lost in thought of the good old days. Those would have been any time Caleb and I were together. As some twins are, we were inseparable growing up. All the way through high school we were always together. We took the same classes, much to the confusion of our teachers. Both of us were on the football team, Caleb was the left tackle and I was the right. When we dated, it was almost always a double date. We joined the Marine Corp together as well and went through basic training at Recruit Training Depot at Paris Island in South Carolina. Following basic, we both were deployed to Afghanistan to fight the war against the Taliban.

We both served two tours ending up just outside of Kabul. A short time before our tour ended, Caleb stepped on an IED and died instantly.

I had been on a recon mission, almost ten miles from where he died. When he died, I died with him. I don't mean that figuratively. At exactly the same time Caleb passed, my body shut down. I was told by the corpsman who brought me back, I had stopped breathing and I had no pulse. The corpsman brought me back to life, stabilized my vitals and rushed me to a field hospital in Kabul. It took me almost a full week to regain consciousness.

When I awoke, a chaplain was standing by my bed and told me that Caleb had been killed. I was confused, because, after all, I was Caleb.

They shipped me back to the states and hospitalized me in a mental institution. It took months of therapy for me to fully realize I wasn't Caleb. At different times I thought I was Joshua, at other times, Caleb. Sometimes, I was sure I was both of us together in the same body.

I was diagnosed as schizophrenic with a multiple personality disorder and placed on heavy medication. The meds turned me into a zombie until one night Caleb said to me, "Bro get up…Man you gotta get up. Right now. We gotta leave this place. They're killing us. They have no idea who we are."

So we stole some scrubs, a lab coat and as many wallets as we could find in the employee locker room and ran away from the funny farm. When I finally got the meds out of my system, things began to clear up. It took us several days but we finally managed to make it back to Georgia. We were sitting in a corner booth in an IHOP in Atlanta and Caleb explained it to me.

"Bro, this is going to sound…unbelievable but I swear to you it's the truth. When I stepped on that IED outside of Kabul, I died instantly but somehow, my consciousness survived and it now shares your brain." I'd gotten used to hearing Caleb's voice in my head by then but it took me a long time to be able to answer him without speaking. Caleb pointed out that talking to imaginary people might be a bit upsetting to those around me, so he had me wear a plug in my ear. It looked like I was carrying on a cell phone conversation.

By this time, we usually conversed silently but the shock of Caleb's comments forced me to shout out loud, "No way!!! You've got to be kidding me! You're not real, you're just some kind of hallucination. You can't really be Caleb. Are you saying you're a ghost? If you are, get the hell out of my head!"

That brought about several strange looks by customers as well as servers. The restaurant manager came over and asked me to leave, the meal was on the house.

We sat on the bench at a bus stop. I had calmed down by then and Caleb continued. "I'm not a ghost, Josh. I'm a spirit. I'm not always in your head. Sometimes, I'm…somewhere else."

"Somewhere else?" I thought "Where exactly, somewhere else?"

"I'd like to tell you, but I can't. I really don't know how to describe it. Most of the time you will be by yourself, but if you ever need me just think my name and I will be there."

It was twilight now and I walked away from the window and laid down on the bed. I thought about how that evening changed my life forever. I was a different person, a better person when Caleb was with me. It felt like I was twice as strong, twice as smart, able to know the right thing at the right time. Having Caleb with me inspired me to do things I never imagined I could do before.

I had been given a medical discharge because of the trauma I had gone through. I knew I could never tell anyone about how Caleb and I had…I guess merged is the best way to describe it. If I ever told anyone they would think I was Looney Tunes.

Caleb directed me to the VA. They had a department that helped vets explore possible job opportunities. They gave us a battery of tests. Then they gave us more tests, all kinds of tests, intelligence tests, physical tests and tests to see how intuitive we were. You name it, they had a test for it. One thing led to another and after a couple of months they ran out of tests. They told us to wait.

Two days later, I received a call asking us to come to a certain location for a job interview. We were picked up by a limo with blackout windows, there was a curtain that separated the driver from us and I tried to speak with him to find out where we were going. When I got no reply, I slid the curtain back. The front of the car was empty.

A disembodied voice said, "Good morning, Joshua. Please sit back and enjoy the ride. Help yourself to the refreshments. Your trip will take approximately forty-three minutes. If you would like music please select from the menu after I have finished my message. Enjoy the ride. This message is complete."

A flat panel display in the back of the no-driver's seat came to life with an extensive list of music available. I ignored it and after a minute the screen went dark.

Caleb? I thought.

"Here bro," he answered inside my head.

"What's going on?"

"We're finally going to get a shot at doing something meaningful. Like the computer said, sit back and enjoy the ride. Nothing to worry about."

So I sat back, selected some Steppenwolf on the really great sound system, opened an ice cold Coke Zero and ate a couple of bags of dry roasted peanuts. Forty-three minutes later the limo came to a stop and the car door automatically opened.

We were inside a very large garage with a moving light display showing me the way to the building's entrance. When I got to the security door, the same voice from the limo said, "Please place your right hand on the scanner."

I complied and felt the warmth of the scanner light as it ran from my finger tips to my wrist. "Thank you, Joshua. Now please look into the retinal scanner with your right eye."

When the scan was complete, the voice said, "Identification confirmed." There was a soft beep and the security door slide quietly open. "Please enter the second door on your left. Enjoy your meeting."

"Thank you," I said.

Immediately Caleb was in my head, "Bro! Why are you thanking a computer?" There was a mirthful tone to his voice.

"I was just being polite," I answered sheepishly. "Force of habit."

The second door on the left opened automatically as I reached for the handle. I waited until the door was fully opened and I could see inside. The room was small with a round table in the middle with four comfortable chairs surrounding the table. There was only one person in the room. He stood as I walked in and extended his hand. He was about six-feet tall, a mature white man in his sixties dressed in a dark blue business suit. He looked well built. His gray hair, what hair he had, was cut high and tight. He had the bearing of a Marine. His handshake was strong, not a bone-crusher grip but very firm.

"Hello, Joshua. Come in and take a seat. I'll have you out of here in an hour."

He was true to his word, an hour later he had finished his briefing. Before I said anything, I checked with Caleb. "What do you think, Bro?"

Caleb's response was immediate, "This is the chance of a life time. Just do it, Josh. I'll be with you all the way."

I signed the paper and we were committed. He never told me his name, he said to call him boss or leader. He was going to be our handler, our single point of contact. Whatever we needed to get the job done, he would provide us.

We went through six months of extensive training before they were ready to turn us loose. Our first mission was in Nogales, Arizona. When that mission was successfully completed, we were given a more complicated mission in Portland, Oregon. When that wrapped up, we moved on to an even more complicated mission in Jericho, Mississippi, that nearly cost me my life.

I was getting sleepy but wanted to talk to my brother.

"Caleb, are you there?"

"Right here, Josh. What's up?"

"Do you think there are others like us?"

"I know there are. Not many but there are some."

"Are they always twins?"

"No, not always but it seems to always be between family members."

"Are they always good people?"

There was a pause and I thought he had left me. Then he answered, "As far as I know, people like us are always the good guys. And more are coming every day. Go to sleep, bro. Happy vacation. I'll be in touch."

As I drifted off to sleep, I realized for the first time, he was my divine intervention. He's the one who inspired me to buy the lightning rods and subtly inspired me for so many other things. I knew he wasn't an angel but he was the closest thing to a guardian angel I would ever have.

My last thoughts as sleep began to shut down my mind were how much I was looking forward to our next mission. I knew Caleb was too. We were born to be the Angels of Death, the punishers of evil. I know I couldn't have survived that last mission without some outstanding help. Having my twin with me was a huge plus. We were together again doing something worthwhile. So if you're one of the many evil people in this world, watch out. We're coming to get you.

This is Frank G. Davis. This concludes the book of <u>Joshua</u>, the first book in the <u>Joshua</u> series. If you enjoyed the book please send me an email at:

<u>sciencefictionfrank@gmail.com</u>

and let me know what you think of the story. I promise to reply to all emails and give you updates on the next books in the series, titled <u>Joshua and Caleb</u>, and <u>The Book of Caleb.</u>

ABOUT THE AUTHOR

I've been a fan of science fiction ever since I was in grade school (a very long time ago). In those days there were three outstanding authors: Isaac Asimov, Arthur C. Clark, and Robert A. Heinlein.

My favorite author was Heinlein. He began writing his science fiction stories for young people. His first books were categorized as 'Boys Books.' Today, they're called 'Young Adults.' His stories were very believable to me and I couldn't wait to get to his latest books. As I matured, so did his books. I have read every book Heinlein published and still have most of them in my personal library. I think my all-time favorite Heinlein story is *Stranger in a Strange Land.*

My current favorite author is Orson Scott Card. Again, like Heinlein's stories, I find myself 'living' the story as it unfolds. *Ender's Game* and *Prentice Alvin* are two of my favorite Card novels.

I've always had an interest in writing science fiction novels. I would read books by new authors and say to myself, "I could write a better story." However, when I tried, publishers didn't agree. When Covid-19 broke out, I had a lot of spare time on my hands and decided to give it another shot.

During the last two years, I have written seven novels with an eighth one in the works. And I'm just getting started.

MORE BOOKS FROM
FRANK G. DAVIS

The Generations Trilogy: